THANKSGIVING COOKBOOK

100 Recipes for a Yummylicious Thanksgiving

Disclaimer

No part of this eBook can be transmitted or reproduced in any form including print, electronic, photocopying, scanning, mechanical or recording without prior written permission from the author.

While the author has taken utmost efforts to ensure the accuracy of the written content, all readers are advised to follow information mentioned herein at their own risk. The author cannot be held responsible for any personal or commercial damage caused by misinterpretation of information. All readers are encouraged to seek professional advice when needed.

What You Will Find In This Book?

Have you been planning this Thanksgivings meal to be one of the best Thanksgivings of all time? If you are, then this recipe book will be exactly what you have been looking for. A recipe book filled with tried and tested Thanksgiving recipes that will leave your family and guests reaching for heaping second and third helpings.

As this holiday approaches closer, the thought of all the warm and delicious meals bring a feeling of excitement and anticipation in everyone. Give your family and guests the meal of their Thanksgiving dreams using the recipes in this book. Prepare the most mouthwatering dishes that are not only delicious but also simple and quick. These recipes include:

1. Roasted turkey

2. Turkey Adorned With Swiss Panini

3. Yams

4. Mashed Potatoes

5. Warm Delicate Pears

6. Crusted Red Onions and Pears

Go ahead and take a look at the recipes which will make you the star chef amongst your friends and family.

Contents

Disclaimer 2

What You Will Find In This Book? 3

Thanksgiving Breakfast Recipes 20

  Holiday Pumpkin Pancakes 20

    Serving Size 20

    Nutritional Facts (Values per Serving) 20

    Ingredients 20

    Preparation Method 20

  Pumpkin and Buttermilk Waffles with Maple Syrup 22

    Serving Size 22

    Nutritional Facts (Values per Serving) 22

    Ingredients 22

    Preparation Method 22

  Cheesy Potato Pancakes 24

    Serving Size 24

    Nutritional Facts (Values per Serving) 24

    Ingredients 24

    Preparation Method 24

  Glazed Meaty Wraps 25

    Serving Size 25

    Nutritional Facts (Values per Serving) 25

    Ingredients 25

    Preparation Method 25

  Thanksgiving Special - Ham Quiche 26

    Serving Size 26

    Nutritional Facts (Values per Serving) 26

    Ingredients 26

    Preparation Method 26

  Cheesy Frittata 28

    Serving Size 28

    Nutritional Facts (Values per Serving) 28

    Ingredients 28

    Preparation Method 28

Fluffy Pumpkin Muffins 30

    Serving Size 30

    Nutritional Facts (Values per Serving)...30

    Ingredients 30

    Preparation Method 30

Mom's Cranberry Pancakes 32

    Serving Size 32

    Nutritional Facts (Values per Serving)...32

    Ingredients 32

    Preparation Method 32

Cheese and Chili Torta 34

    Serving Size 34

    Nutritional Facts (Values per Serving)...34

    Ingredients 34

    Preparation Method 34

Spicy Turkey Patties 36

    Serving Size 36

    Nutritional Facts (Values per Serving)...36

    Ingredients 36

    Preparation Method 36

Special Pumpkin Latte 38

    Serving Size 38

    Nutritional Facts (Values per Serving)...38

    Ingredients 38

    Preparation Method 38

Thanksgiving Breakfast Platter 39

    Serving Size 39

    Nutritional Facts (Values per Serving)...39

    Ingredients for Potato Hash 39

    Ingredients for Turkey Crumble...39

    Ingredients for Omelet 39

    Ingredients to Garnish 40

    Preparation Method 40

Pumpkin Bites...41

6

Serving Size 41

Nutritional Facts (Values per Serving).. 41

Ingredients for Pumpkin Bites 41

Ingredients for Spice Glaze 41

Ingredients for Sugar Glaze 42

Preparation Method.. 42

Chicken and Ham Casserole 44

Serving Size 44

Nutritional Facts (Values per Serving).. 44

Ingredients 44

Preparation Method.. 44

Honey Nut Filled Baklava 45

Serving Size 45

Nutritional Facts (Values per Serving).. 45

Ingredients 45

Ingredients for Sauce 45

Ingredients for Nut Filling 45

Preparation Method.. 45

Holiday Coffee 47

Serving Size 47

Nutritional Facts (Values per Serving).. 47

Ingredients 47

Preparation Method.. 47

Cheese Lovers Breakfast 48

Serving Size 48

Nutritional Facts (Values per Serving).. 48

Ingredients 48

Preparation Method.. 48

Cranberry Crumble 50

Serving Size 50

Nutritional Facts (Values per Serving).. 50

Ingredients 50

Preparation Method.. 50

Thanksgiving Appetizers 51

Spread with Smoked Trout 51

    Serving Size 51

    Nutritional Facts (Values per Serving) 51

    Ingredients 51

    Preparation Method 51

Pistachios, Brie and Roasted Pears 53

    Serving Size 53

    Nutritional Facts (Values per Serving) 53

    Ingredients 53

    Preparation Method 53

Cheesy Nut Balls 55

    Serving Size 55

    Nutritional Facts (Values per Serving) 55

    Ingredients 55

    Preparation Method 55

Canapés with Apricots 57

    Serving Size 57

    Nutritional Facts (Values per Serving) 57

    Ingredients 57

    Preparation Method 57

Mousse With Liver and Chicken 58

    Serving Size 58

    Nutritional Facts (Values per Serving) 58

    Ingredients 58

    Preparation Method 58

Spicy Mississippian Pecans 60

    Serving Size 60

    Nutritional Facts (Values per Serving) 60

    Ingredients 60

    Preparation Method 60

Spread with Ham 61

    Serving Size 61

    Nutritional Facts (Values per Serving) 61

    Ingredients 61

Preparation Method..61

Scandinavian Treats...62

    Serving Size...62

    Nutritional Facts (Values per Serving)..62

    Ingredients...62

    Preparation Method..62

Special Thanksgiving Sauce..63

    Serving Size...63

    Nutritional Facts (Values per Serving)..63

    Ingredients...63

    Preparation Method..63

Berrylicious Sauce..64

    Serving Size...64

    Nutritional Facts (Values per Serving)..64

    Ingredients...64

    Preparation Method..64

Green Meat Soup with Toast...65

    Serving Size...65

    Nutritional Facts (Values per Serving)..65

    Ingredients...65

    Preparation Method..65

Quick and Light Meatball Soup..67

    Serving Size...67

    Nutritional Facts (Values per Serving)..67

    Ingredients...67

    Preparation Method..67

Fall Special – Bean Soup..68

    Serving Size...68

    Nutritional Facts (Values per Serving)..68

    Ingredients...68

    Preparation Method..68

Chicken Tortilla Stew..70

    Serving Size...70

    Nutritional Facts (Values per Serving)..70

Ingredients 70

Preparation Method 71

Thanksgiving Salads and Sidelines 72

Pink Salad with Cranberries 72

Serving Size 72

Nutritional Facts (Values per Serving)..72

Ingredients 72

Preparation Method 72

Onions with Creamed Peas 73

Serving Size 73

Nutritional Facts (Values per Serving)..73

Ingredients 73

Preparation Method 73

Onions and Spinach Salad 74

Serving Size 74

Nutritional Facts (Values per Serving)..74

Ingredients 74

Preparation Method 74

Garlic-Y Mashed Potatoes...76

Serving Size 76

Nutritional Facts (Values per Serving)..76

Ingredients 76

Preparation Method 76

Simple Salad with Pearl Onions 77

Serving Size 77

Nutritional Facts (Values per Serving)..77

Ingredients 77

Preparation Method 77

Turnip Salad 78

Serving Size 78

Nutritional Facts (Values per Serving)..78

Ingredients 78

Preparation Method 78

Spicy Green Salad 80

Serving Size 80

Nutritional Facts (Values per Serving) 80

Ingredients 80

Preparation Method 80

Mashed Potatoes 82

Serving Size 82

Nutritional Facts (Values per Serving) 82

Ingredients 82

Preparation Method 82

Cranberry and Walnut Stuffing 83

Serving Size 83

Nutritional Facts (Values per Serving) 83

Ingredients 83

Preparation Method 83

Thanksgiving Lunch 84

Healthy Bean Casserole 84

Serving Size 84

Nutritional Facts (Values per Serving) 84

Ingredients 84

Preparation Method 84

Roasted Thanksgiving Turkey 86

Serving Size 86

Nutritional Facts (Values per Serving) 86

Ingredients for Turkey 86

Ingredients for Glaze 86

Preparation Method 86

Warm Delicate Pear 88

Serving Size 88

Nutritional Facts (Values per Serving) 88

Ingredients 88

Preparation Method 88

Turkey Stuffing 89

Serving Size 89

Nutritional Facts (Values per Serving) 89

Ingredients 89

Preparation Method 89

Sweet Potatoes Delight 91

Serving Size 91

Nutritional Facts (Values per Serving) 91

Ingredients for Potatoes 91

Ingredients for Topping 91

Preparation Method 91

Sugar, Spice and Everything Nice Turkey 93

Serving Size 93

Nutritional Facts (Values per Serving) 93

Ingredients 93

Preparation Method 93

Lemonized Green Beans 95

Serving Size 95

Nutritional Facts (Values per Serving) 95

Ingredients 95

Preparation Method 95

Herbilicious Turkey 96

Serving Size 96

Nutritional Facts (Values per Serving) 96

Ingredients 96

Preparation Method 96

Thanksgiving Cheese Balls 98

Serving Size 98

Nutritional Facts (Values per Serving) 98

Ingredients 98

Preparation Method 98

Crusted Red Onions and Pears 99

Serving Size 99

Nutritional Facts (Values per Serving) 99

Ingredients 99

Preparation Method 99

Roasted Tomatoes with Baked Ziti 101

Serving Size 101

Nutritional Facts (Values per Serving) 101

Ingredients 101

Preparation Method 101

Thanksgiving-Y Tortellini 103

Serving Size 103

Nutritional Facts (Values per Serving) 103

Ingredients 103

Preparation Method 103

Turkey gravy 105

Serving Size 105

Nutritional Facts (Values per Serving) 105

Ingredients 105

Preparation Method 105

Turkey Adorned With Swiss Panini 106

Serving Size 106

Nutritional Facts (Values per Serving) 106

Ingredients 106

Preparation Method 106

Dried Turkey with Rosemary 107

Serving Size 107

Nutritional Facts (Values per Serving) 107

Ingredients 107

Preparation Method 107

Thanksgiving Celebration Cocktails 109

Martini with Pears 109

Serving Size 109

Nutritional Facts (Values per Serving) 109

Ingredients 109

Preparation Method 109

Spicy and Gingery Cocktail 110

Serving Size 110

Nutritional Facts (Values per Serving) 110

Ingredients 110

Preparation Method 110

Kings Cider 111

    Serving Size 111

    Nutritional Facts (Values per Serving) 111

    Ingredients 111

    Preparation Method 111

Martini with Caramel Apple Pies 112

    Serving Size 112

    Nutritional Facts (Values per Serving) 112

    Ingredients 112

    Preparation Method 112

Thanksgiving Margaritas 113

    Serving Size 113

    Nutritional Facts (Values per Serving) 113

    Ingredients 113

    Preparation Method 113

Cider and Butterscotch 114

    Serving Size 114

    Nutritional Facts (Values per Serving) 114

    Ingredients 114

    Preparation Method 114

Almond-Y Cocktail 115

    Serving Size 115

    Nutritional Facts (Values per Serving) 115

    Ingredients 115

    Preparation Method 115

Cognac Cosmopolitan 116

    Serving Size 116

    Nutritional Facts (Values per Serving) 116

    Ingredients 116

    Preparation Method 116

Apple Cinnamon Drink 117

    Serving Size 117

    Nutritional Facts (Values per Serving) 117

Ingredients 117

Preparation Method 117

Thanksgiving Rum 118

Serving Size 118

Nutritional Facts (Values per Serving) 118

Ingredients 118

Preparation Method 118

Vodka with a Herb-Y Tinge 119

Serving Size 119

Nutritional Facts (Values per Serving) 119

Ingredients 119

Preparation Method 119

Thanksgiving Dinner 120

Spicy and Smoky Turkey 120

Serving Size 120

Nutritional Facts (Values per Serving) 120

Ingredients 120

Preparation Method 120

Sausage and Apple Stuffing With Wild Rice 122

Serving Size 122

Nutritional Facts (Values per Serving) 122

Ingredients 122

Preparation Method 122

Brined Turkey 124

Serving Size 124

Nutritional Facts (Values per Serving) 124

Ingredients 124

Preparation Method 124

Maple-D Sweet Potatoes 126

Serving Size 126

Nutritional Facts (Values per Serving) 126

Ingredients 126

Preparation Method 126

Yummilicious Turkey with Apple Cider 127

Serving Size 127

Nutritional Facts (Values per Serving) 127

Ingredients 127

Preparation Method 128

Casseroles with Mixed Vegetables 129

Serving Size 129

Nutritional Facts (Values per Serving) 129

Ingredients 129

Preparation Method 129

Zesty Turkey 130

Serving Size 130

Nutritional Facts (Values per Serving) 130

Ingredients 130

Preparation Method 130

Good Well Roasted Turkey 132

Serving Size 132

Nutritional Facts (Values per Serving) 132

Ingredients 132

Preparation Method 132

Sage and Chestnuts with Brussels sprouts 134

Serving Size 134

Nutritional Facts (Values per Serving) 134

Ingredients 134

Preparation Method 134

Juicy Turkey 135

Serving Size 135

Nutritional Facts (Values per Serving) 135

Ingredients 135

Preparation Method 135

Turkey Burgers 137

Serving Size 137

Nutritional Facts (Values per Serving) 137

Ingredients 137

Preparation Method 137

Turkey Calzone...138

    Serving Size...138

    Nutritional Facts (Values per Serving)...138

    Ingredients 138

    Preparation Method...138

Delicata With Onions and Squash 139

    Serving Size...139

    Nutritional Facts (Values per Serving)...139

    Ingredients 139

    Preparation Method...139

Oven-ized Turkey 141

    Serving Size...141

    Nutritional Facts (Values per Serving)...141

    Ingredients 141

    Preparation Method...141

Crockpot Turkey 143

    Serving Size...143

    Nutritional Facts (Values per Serving)...143

    Ingredients 143

    Preparation Method...143

Grilly Turkey 144

    Serving Size...144

    Nutritional Facts (Values per Serving)...144

    Ingredients 144

    Preparation Method...144

Thanksgiving Special Deserts 146

Marmalade Celebration Cheesecake 146

    Serving Size...146

    Nutritional Facts (Values per Serving)...146

    Ingredients 146

    Preparation Method...147

Low Fat Pear Cheesecake 149

    Serving Size...149

    Nutritional Facts (Values per Serving)...149

Ingredients 149

Preparation Method 149

Crunchy Pumpkin Mousse 151

Serving Size 151

Nutritional Facts (Values per Serving)... 151

Ingredients 151

Preparation Method 151

Nutty Pear Treat 153

Serving Size 153

Nutritional Facts (Values per Serving)... 153

Ingredients 153

Preparation Method 153

Lavender Strawberries with Cream Dip 155

Serving Size 155

Nutritional Facts (Values per Serving)... 155

Ingredients 155

Preparation Method 155

Chewy Fudge Brownies 157

Serving Size 157

Nutritional Facts (Values per Serving)... 157

Ingredients 157

Preparation Method 157

Lemon Catalana 159

Serving Size 159

Nutritional Facts (Values per Serving)... 159

Ingredients 159

Preparation Method 159

Chocolicious Bundt Cake 161

Serving Size 161

Nutritional Facts (Values per Serving)... 161

Ingredients 161

Preparation Method 162

Low Fat Squash Cheesecake 163

Serving Size 163

Nutritional Facts (Values per Serving)..163

Ingredients 163

Preparation Method..163

Coconut Flavored Pumpkin Pie 165

Serving Size 165

Nutritional Facts (Values per Serving)..165

Ingredients for Crust...165

Ingredients for Filling..165

Preparation Method..166

Crunchy Thanksgiving Cake Delight..167

Serving Size 167

Nutritional Facts (Values per Serving)..167

Ingredients 167

Preparation Method..167

Creamy Pumpkin Cake Roll..169

Serving Size 169

Nutritional Facts (Values per Serving)..169

Ingredients for Cake roll 169

Ingredients for Filling..169

Preparation Method..169

Spicy Pumpkin Treat...171

Serving Size 171

Nutritional Facts (Values per Serving)..171

Ingredients 171

Preparation Method..171

Choco Pumpkin Cookies 173

Serving Size 173

Nutritional Facts (Values per Serving)..173

Ingredients 173

Preparation Method..173

Breadilicious Pumpkin Pudding 175

Serving Size 175

Nutritional Facts (Values per Serving)..175

Ingredients 175

Preparation Method 175

Low Fat Pumpkin Butter 177

    Serving Size 177

    Nutritional Facts (Values per Serving) 177

    Ingredients 177

    Preparation Method 177

Pumpkin Pie Spice 179

    Serving Size 179

    Nutritional Facts (Values per Serving) 179

    Ingredients 179

    Preparation Method 179

Final Words 180

Thanksgiving Breakfast Recipes

Holiday Pumpkin Pancakes

Serving Size

Serves 4

Nutritional Facts (Values per Serving)

Calories/serving: 273

Total Carbohydrate: 42.2 g

Cholesterol: 64.9 mg

Total Fat: 8.2 g

Ingredients

All purpose flour – 1 ¼ cups

Canned pumpkin puree - 6 Tbsp

Milk – 1 cup

Egg - 1

Ginger powder - 1/2 tsp

Melted Butter - 2 Tbsp

Cinnamon - 1/2 tsp

Baking powder - 2 tsp

Clove - 1 pinch

Sugar - 2 Tbsp

Nutmeg - 1/2 tsp

Salt - 1/2 tsp

Oil to grease the pan

Preparation Method

7. Mix all-purpose flour, baking powder, sugar, salt, clove, nutmeg, cinnamon and ginger powder in a large bowl.

8. In another bowl, whisk egg, milk, melted butter and pumpkin puree.

9. Fold the dry mixture in the pumpkin mixture.

10. Grease a skillet with any cooking oil.

11. Heat the skillet over medium heat.

12. Pour about a quarter cup batter in the skillet for each pancake.

13. Cook for 3 -4 minutes per side.

14. Serve with maple syrup.

Pumpkin and Buttermilk Waffles with Maple Syrup

Serving Size

Serves 6

Nutritional Facts (Values per Serving)

Calories/serving: 195

Total Carbohydrate: 28.2 g

Cholesterol: 325 mg

Total Fat: 6.2 g

Ingredients

All-Purpose Flour - 4 Cups

Baking Powder - 1 tsp

Whole Wheat Flour - Half Cup

Eggs - 2

Canned Pumpkin- Half cup

Brown Sugar - 2 Tbsp

Baking Soda – ¼ tsp

Buttermilk – 1¼ cups

Ground Cinnamon - 1 tsp

Melted Butter – 2 Tbsp

Ground Ginger - Half tsp

Ground Cloves - ¼ tsp

Salt - ¼ tsp

Maple syrup to serve

Preparation Method

1. In a large bowl, mix all-purpose flour, whole wheat flour, brown sugar, baking powder, ground cinnamon, ground ginger, baking soda, salt and ground cloves.

2. In another bowl, whisk eggs, pumpkin puree, buttermilk and melted butter.

3. Fold the dry mixture in the pumpkin mixture.

4. Pour about half a cup batter in a preheated waffle iron.

5. Cook until it become golden brown.

6. Serve with maple syrup.

Cheesy Potato Pancakes

Serving Size

Serves 4

Nutritional Facts (Values per Serving)

Calories/serving: 267

Total Carbohydrate: 49 g

Cholesterol: 97 mg

Total Fat: 3.7 g

Ingredients

Mashed potatoes – 4 cups

Cheddar Cheese, grated - 1 cup

Eggs - 3

Flour – Half cup

1 small onion - Finely chopped

Crushed garlic – 1 tsp

Cooking oil for frying

Salt to taste

Black pepper to taste

Preparation Method

1. In a large bowl, mix well all the ingredients except for oil.

2. Put a few tablespoons of cooking oil in a skillet.

3. Let the oil get hot.

4. Pour about half a cup mixture to make each pancake.

5. Cook for 3 minutes per side.

Enjoy!

Glazed Meaty Wraps

Serving Size

Serves 10 – 12

Nutritional Facts (Values per Serving)

Calories/serving: 294

Total Carbohydrate: 14.3 g

Cholesterol: 62 mg

Total Fat: 18.7 g

Ingredients

Chicken breasts, skinless and boneless – 1½ lbs

Sliced bacon – 1 lb

Brown sugar – 1 cup

Red chili powder – 2 Tbsp

Salt to taste

Preparation Method

1. Cut the chicken breast in 1-inch cubes.

2. Set the oven to preheat at 350°F.

3. Cut each bacon slice into three equal parts.

4. Wrap 1 chicken cube in one part of the bacon slice.

5. Insert a toothpick diagonally to secure bacon to the chicken cube.

6. In a tray, mix the brown sugar, salt and chili powder.

7. Coat the wrapped chicken in this dry rub.

8. Grease a broiler pan with a non-stick cooking spray.

9. Put all the wrapped chicken cubes in the greased broiler pan.

10. Put the pan in the preheated oven for 30 minutes or until the bacon is completely cooked.

Thanksgiving Special - Ham Quiche

Serving Size

Serves 10 – 12

Nutritional Facts (Values per Serving)

Calories/serving: 153

Total Carbohydrate: 4.6 g

Cholesterol: 84.2 mg

Total Fat: 12.3 g

Ingredients

Cooked ham, shredded – 1 cup

Eggs - 3

Baking mix – Half cup

Cheddar cheese, shredded – Half cup

Melted butter – ¼ cup

Ripe olives – Half cup

Parmesan cheese, grated – 2 Tbsp

Hot pepper sauce -1/2 tsp

Ground mustard - Half tsp

Preparation Method

1. Set the oven to preheat at 375oF.

2. Grease 12 muffin cups.

3. In a large bowl, mix ham, olives and cheddar cheese.

4. Divide this mixture in the greased muffin cups.

5. In another bowl, mix well all the remaining ingredients.

6. Pour the mixture equally on top of all the muffin cups.

7. Put the cups in the oven for 25 – 30 minutes.

Cheesy Frittata

Serving Size

Serves 4

Nutritional Facts (Values per Serving)

Calories/serving: 183.4

Total Carbohydrate: 4.2 g

Cholesterol: 228 mg

Total Fat: 11.3 g

Ingredients

Romano cheese, grated - Half Cup

Egg whites of 6 eggs

4 whole eggs

Plum tomatoes, finely sliced – 2

Fresh sage, chopped – 1 tsp

Green onions, sliced – 2 medium sized

Zucchini, sliced – 1 small sized

Olive Oil – 1 tsp

Salt – ½ tsp

Pepper – ¼ tsp

Preparation Method

1. In a large mixing bowl, whisk the whole eggs, egg whites, eggs, half of the Romano cheese, sage, salt and pepper.

2. Grease a 10-inch deep oven proof skillet with cooking spray.

3. Sauté zucchini and onions in it for 2 -3 minutes.

4. Put the egg mixture in the skillet.

5. Cover the pan and let it cook on medium heat for 5 minutes.

6. Remove the lid

7. Spread the tomato slices and the remaining Romano cheese in the skillet.

8. Broil for 4 – 5 minutes or until eggs are completely set.

9. Cut into wedges and serve.

Fluffy Pumpkin Muffins

Serving Size

Serves 10 - 12

Nutritional Facts (Values per Serving)

Calories/serving: 248.7

Total Carbohydrate: 35.8 g

Cholesterol: 83.7 mg

Total Fat: 10.4 g

Ingredients

Unsalted butter – Half cup

Eggs - 4

Brown sugar – ¾ cup

Whole wheat flour – 1½ cup

Milk – Half cup

Canned Pumpkin – 15 oz.

Yellow cornmeal - 1 cup

Ground cinnamon – 1 tsp

Baking powder – 2 tsp

Ground cloves - ½ tsp

Baking soda – 1 tsp

Salt - ½ tsp

Cooking oil to grease the pan

Preparation Method

1. Set the oven to preheat at 350oF.

2. Grease the muffin pan with cooking oil

3. In a mixing bowl, whisk the butter and brown sugar till it becomes light and fluffy.

4. Add the remaining ingredients in the same bowl and beat well.

5. Pour the batter in the greased muffin pan.

6. Put it in the preheated oven for 30 – 35 minutes.

Mom's Cranberry Pancakes

Serving Size

Serves 4 – 6

Nutritional Facts (Values per Serving)

Calories/serving: 494

Total Carbohydrate: 71 g

Cholesterol: 136 mg

Total Fat: 17.8 g

Ingredients

Milk – ¾ cup

Sugar – 2½ tsp

Egg - 1

Melted butter – 2 Tbsp

Flour – 1 cup

Baking powder - 2 tsp

Fresh or frozen cranberries – Half cup

Salt – ½ tsp

Preparation Method

1. In a large bowl, whisk egg, milk and melted butter.

2. In another bowl, mix baking powder, flour, 2 tablespoons sugar and salt.

3. Mix the dry mixture in the egg mixture.

4. Cut the cranberries in half.

5. Mix the half cut cranberries with the remaining sugar in microwave safe bowl.

6. Microwave on high till the cranberries starts to bubble. Stop the microwave and stir the cranberries after every 15 seconds.

7. Mix the hot cranberries in the batter.

8. Grease a pan with butter or cooking oil.

9. Pour about half cup batter to make each pancake.

10. Cook for 3 – 4 minutes per side.

Serve with maple syrup.

Cheese and Chili Torta

Serving Size

Serves 4 – 5

Nutritional Facts (Values per Serving)

Calories/serving: 715

Total Carbohydrate: 17.5 g

Cholesterol: 380 mg

Total Fat: 53.8 g

Ingredients

Cheddar cheese, grated – ½ lb

Eggs - 5

Monterey jack cheese, grated – ½ lb

Picante sauce – ¼ cup

Cream - 1 ½ cup

Flour – 1/3 cup

Green chilies, canned – 4 oz.

Preparation Method

1. Set the oven to preheat at 370oF.

2. Grease a 10-inch deep pie plate with butter.

3. In a bowl, mix both the cheeses.

4. Spread the cheese mixture evenly in the greased pie plate.

5. Whisk eggs. Add half of the flour in it. Beat well.

6. Add the remaining flour and beat well.

7. Pour this egg mixture over the cheese in the pie plate.

8. Spread chilies on top.

9. Top it up with picante sauce.

10. Put it in the preheated oven for 40 – 45 minutes.

Spicy Turkey Patties

Serving Size

Serves 4 – 6

Nutritional Facts (Values per Serving)

Calories/serving: 175.3

Total Carbohydrate: 1.5 g

Cholesterol: 78.4 mg

Total Fat: 8.9 g

Ingredients

Ground turkey -1 lb

Fennel Seed – 1 tsp

Garlic powder – ½ tsp

Thyme – 1 tsp

Ground cloves – 1/8 tsp

Nutmeg – 1/8 tsp

Black Pepper – 1 tsp

Cayenne Pepper – ½ tsp

Allspice – 1/8 tsp

Salt – 1 tsp

White pepper – ½ tsp

Sage – 2 tsp

Cooking Oil for frying

Preparation Method

1. In a large bowl, mix all the ingredients.

2. Make medium sized patties out of it.

3. Heat cooking oil in a skillet over low to medium heat.

4. One by one, shallow fry patties in it till the meat is fully cooked.

Serve with bread and tomato ketchup.

Special Pumpkin Latte

Serving Size

Serves 4

Nutritional Facts (Values per Serving)

Calories/serving: 202

Total Carbohydrate: 29.7 g

Cholesterol: 20.4 mg

Total Fat: 5.1 g

Ingredients

Pumpkin Puree – 1 cup

Milk – 1 quart

Cinnamon powder – 1 tsp

White Sugar - ¼ cup

Vanilla extract – 1 Tbsp

Preparation Method

1. Put all the ingredients in a large saucepan.

2. Cook over medium heat till the mixture comes to a simmer. Do not bring it to boil.

3. Whisk it while cooking to make it frothy.

Serve it hot.

Thanksgiving Breakfast Platter

Serving Size

Serves 3 - 4

Nutritional Facts (Values per Serving)

Calories/serving: 485.5

Total Carbohydrate: 29.1 g

Cholesterol: 465 mg

Total Fat: 33.1 g

Ingredients for Potato Hash

1 egg – whisked with 1 tablespoon water

Mashed potatoes – 2 cups

Canola oil – 2 Tbsp

Bread crumbs – Half cup

Salt and pepper to taste

Ingredients for Turkey Crumble

Cooked turkey, diced - 1 cup

White onion, chopped – 1 small sized

Green beans, chopped – Half cup

Canola oil - 1 Tbsp

Red bell pepper, chopped – 1 medium sized

Salt and pepper to taste

Ingredients for Omelet

Eggs - 8

Canola oil – 3 Tbsp

Salt and pepper to taste

Ingredients to Garnish

> Fresh sage, chopped - 2 Tbsp
>
> Parsley, chopped - 2 Tbsp
>
> Thyme, chopped – 2 Tbsp

Preparation Method

To make potato hash,

1. Mix salt, pepper and mashed potatoes.

2. Make 16 patties from it.

3. Dip each patty first in the egg-water mixture than bread crumbs.

4. Heat canola oil in a large skillet.

5. Fry the patties in it over medium – high heat till both sides become golden brown.

To make turkey Crumble,

6. Heat canola oil in a large skillet over medium heat.

7. Sauté onion and bell pepper in it.

8. Add salt and pepper. Stir to mix.

9. Cook for 3 – 4 minutes.

10. Add turkey and green beans in the skillet.

11. Cook for another 3 – 4 minutes.

To make omelets,

12. Whisk eggs in salt and pepper.

13. Fry four large omelets in canola oil.

To serve,

14. Make four plates each having 2 potato hashes, ¼ of the turkey and 1 omelet.

15. Garnish with fresh thyme, parsley and sage.

Pumpkin Bites

Serving Size

Serves 5 – 6

Nutritional Facts (Values per Serving)

Calories/serving: 525

Total Carbohydrate: 95.3 g

Cholesterol: 65 mg

Total Fat: 14 g

Ingredients for Pumpkin Bites

All-purpose flour – 2 cups

Sugar – 7 Tbsp

Baking powder – 1 Tbsp

Salt – ½ tsp

Cinnamon Powder – ½ tsp

Ground nutmeg – ½ tsp

Cloves, crushed – 1/4 tsp

Ginger powder – 1/4 tsp

Butter - 6 Tbsp

Canned pumpkin – Half cup

Egg – 1

Ingredients for Spice Glaze

Castor sugar – 1 cup

Whole milk – 2 Tbsp

Cinnamon Powder – 1/4 tsp

Pinch of ground nutmeg

Ginger powder – 1/4 tsp

Ground cloves – 1/4 tsp

Ingredients for Sugar Glaze

Castor sugar – 1 cup

Whole milk – 2 Tbsp

Preparation Method

To make the pumpkin bites,

1. Set the oven to preheat at 425°F.

2. Line a baking sheet with a parchment paper.

3. In a large bowl, mix flour, baking powder, sugar, salt and all other spices.

4. Cut the butter in small cubes and mix it in the bowl till it all becomes a crumbly mixture. Set aside.

5. In another bowl, whisk egg and pumpkin.

6. Fold the crumbly dry mixture in the wet mixture.

7. Kneed to form a ball of dough.

8. Pat out the dough on a floured surface.

9. Mold it in a 1 inch thick rectangle.

10. Use a pizza cutter or sharp knife to cut the dough in 6 equal slices.

11. Place the dough slices on a baking sheet.

12. Put it in the preheated oven for 15 – 20 minutes.

13. Set aside to cool.

To make the sugar glaze,

14. Mix castor sugar with milk.

15. Whisk till it becomes smooth.

16. When the bites are cool, brush the sugar glaze on every bite.

To make the spice glaze,

17. Mix all the spice glaze ingredients.

18. As the sugar glaze firms up, brush the spice glaze on every bite.

19. Let it sit for 60 minutes before serving.

Chicken and Ham Casserole

Serving Size

Serves 6

Nutritional Facts (Values per Serving)

Calories/serving: 199.5

Total Carbohydrate: 4.3 g

Cholesterol: 517 mg

Total Fat: 13.8 g

Ingredients

Cooked ham, cubed – 1 ½ cups

Dry chicken stove top stuffing mix - 2 cups

Cheddar cheese, shredded – 1 cup

Milk – 2 cups

Eggs, whisked - 6

Salt – Half teaspoon

Preparation Method

1. Set the oven to preheat at 350oF.

2. Grease a baking dish with cooking spray.

3. In a large bowl, mix all the ingredients well.

4. Pour and set the mixture evenly in the greased baking dish.

5. Put it in the preheated oven for 40 – 45 minutes.

Serve it hot!

Honey Nut Filled Baklava

Serving Size

Serves 8

Nutritional Facts (Values per Serving)

Calories/serving: 374.5

Total Carbohydrate: 55.3 g

Cholesterol: 0.0 mg

Total Fat: 15.3 g

Ingredients

Frozen butter biscuits – 16 oz.

Ingredients for Sauce

Honey – half cup

Whole cloves – 3

Lemon juice – 2 tsp

Sugar – ¼ cup

Ground cinnamon – 1/8 tsp

Water – 1/3 cup

Pinch of salt

Ingredients for Nut Filling

Walnut, halves – ¼ cup

Almond, blanched and sliced – half cup

Cinnamon powder – half teaspoon

Sugar – 1 Tbsp

Pinch of salt

Preparation Method

1. Set the oven to preheat at 350°F.

2. Grease eight nonstick muffin cups with nonstick cooking spray

To make the sauce,

3. Mix all the syrup ingredients in a saucepan.

4. Bring it to boil.

5. Remove it from heat and let it sit for 10 minutes.

6. Discard the whole cloves out it.

To make the nut filling,

7. Blend all the nut filling ingredients in a food processor.

8. Blend till all the ingredients are finely chopped.

To make Honey Nut Filled Baklava,

9. Divide the dough equally into 8 biscuits

10. Make 3 layers of each biscuit.

11. Put 1 layer of biscuit at the bottom of each muffin cup.

12. Brush the sauce on top of it.

13. Pour 1 teaspoon nut filling in each muffin cup.

14. Top it off with 1 teaspoon sauce.

15. Put the second layer of biscuit.

16. Repeat the nut filling and syrup layering.

17. Top it off with third layer of biscuit.

18. Put it in the preheated oven for 20 – 25 minutes.

Serve it with the remaining sauce.

Holiday Coffee

Serving Size

Serves 1

Nutritional Facts (Values per Serving)

Calories/serving: 122

Total Carbohydrate: 19.5 g

Cholesterol: 9.1 mg

Total Fat: 1.9 g

Ingredients

Hot coffee – half cup

Milk – ¾ cup

Pumpkin puree – 2 Tbsp

Brown sugar – 2 tsp

Ground nutmeg – ½ tsp

Vanilla extract – ¼ tsp

Pinch of ground ginger

Pinch of ground cinnamon

Preparation Method

1. Put all the ingredients expect for hot coffee in a food processor.

2. Blend till it becomes frothy.

3. Pour the frothy mixture in a saucepan and bring it to boil.

4. Put the hot coffee in a mug.

5. Top it off with hot frothy milk mixture.

Cheese Lovers Breakfast

Serving Size

Serves 10 - 12

Nutritional Facts (Values per Serving)

Calories/serving: 275

Total Carbohydrate: 9 g

Cholesterol: 117 mg

Total Fat: 4.7 g

Ingredients

Cooked bacon, crumbled – 10 slices

Milk – ½ cup

Soft packaged cream cheese – 8 oz.

Blue cheese, crumbled – ¼ cup

Cheddar cheese, grated – 2 cups

White part of green onion, chopped – ¼ cup

Fresh parsley, chopped – ¼ cup

Pecans, chopped – 1 cup (Paula uses Fisher pecans)

Canned Pimientos, drained – 2 oz.

Poppy seeds – 1 Tbsp

Salt and pepper to taste

Preparation Method

1. In a large bowl, beat well the cream cheese and milk.

2. Mix in it the cheddar cheese, blue cheese, pimento, onions, half of the crumbled bacon and half pecans.

3. Add salt and pepper. Mix well.

4. Kneed the mixture in the form of a ball.

5. In a pie plate, mix parsley, poppy seeds and remaining pecans and bacon.

6. Roll the cheese ball into this mixture.

7. Let it sit for a few minutes.

8. Cut into pieces and serve.

Cranberry Crumble

Serving Size

Serves 5 – 6

Nutritional Facts (Values per Serving)

Calories/serving: 67.5

Total Carbohydrate: 11.7 g

Cholesterol: 0.0 mg

Total Fat: 1.7 g

Ingredients

Low fat Greek yogurt – half cup

Honey – 2 tsp

Unsweetened dried cranberries – 2 Tbsp

Unsweetened cranberry juice – half cup

Wheat germ – 1 Tbsp

Steel cut oats – 6 Tbsp

Unsalted sunflower seeds – 1 Tbsp

Vanilla extract – ¼ tsp

Pinch of salt

Preparation Method

1. In a large bowl, mix all the ingredients.

2. You can serve as it is or refrigerate to serve it cold.

Thanksgiving Appetizers

Spread with Smoked Trout

Serving Size

Serves 4

Nutritional Facts (Values per Serving)

Calories/serving: 365

Total Carbohydrate: 59 g

Cholesterol: 23 mg

Total Fat: 9 g

Ingredients

Lemon juice – 3 Tbsp

English cucumber (sliced) – 1

Red onion – Half

Cream cheese (reduced fat) – Half cup

Crackers (whole grain) – 20

Parsley (chopped) – 1 Tbsp

Tomatoes – 2

White beans (cooked or rinsed) – Half cup

Trout (Boned, skinned and smoked) – 4 ounces

Horseradish (prepared) – 1 tbsp

Black pepper – A pinch

Preparation Method

1. Chop about 2 Tbsp of onion and slice the rest.

2. Take a bowl and put mashed beans, cream cheese, chopped onions, lemon juice, trout, parsley, pepper, and horseradish in it. Mix the ingredients well.

3. Garnish the appetizer with sliced onion, tomatoes and cucumber. Serve!

Pistachios, Brie and Roasted Pears

Serving Size

Serves 4

Nutritional Facts (Values per Serving)

Calories/serving: 160

Total Carbohydrate: 18 g

Cholesterol: 14 mg

Total Fat: 9 mg

Ingredients

Salt – Quarter tsp

Extra virgin olive oil – 1 Tbsp

Lemon juice – 1 tsp

Ground pepper – Half tsp

Honey mustard – 2 Tbsp

Pistachios (chopped) – 4 tsp

Pears – 2

Cheese slices – 4

Preparation Method

1. Heat the oven beforehand at 425 Fahrenheit and prepare the baking pan by glazing oil over it.

2. Mix mustard, salt, lemon juice, pepper and oil in a bowl.

3. Flatten the pears by cutting them in half and removing the core part.

4. Take a cooking brush and smear the bowl ingredients all over the pears and keep them in the oven.

5. Let the pears bake for half an hour, take them out and flip the pears. Let them stay in the oven until they are properly baked.

6. Take them out and sprinkle pistachios over them and serve!

Cheesy Nut Balls

Serving Size

Makes 4 dozen balls

Nutritional Facts (Values per Serving)

Calories/serving: 64

Total Carbohydrate: 1 g

Cholesterol: 11 mg

Total Fat: 6 g

Ingredients

Salt – A pinch

Garlic powder – 1 tsp

Onion (grated) – 1 tsp

Pecan (toasted and chopped) – 2 cups

Ground pepper – A pinch

Pimientos (chopped) – 3 Tbsp

Mayonnaise (low fat) – 3 Tbsp

Cheddar cheese – 2 cups

Monterey jack cheese – 2 cups

Cream cheese (low fat) – Quarter cup

Preparation Method

1. Put cream all 3 cheeses in the food processor and run the machine until they all combine well.

2. Include garlic powder, pepper, salt, mayonnaise, onion, pimientos in the food processor and then pulse the ingredients once again.

3. Take out the pulsed ingredients in a bowl and then cover and refrigerate the bowl for approximately 30 minutes.

4. Take out pecans in another bowl.

5. Take a small portion of cheese and roll it to form a ball. Cover it with pecans.

6. Put them in a serving dish and present it to your guests.

Canapés with Apricots

Serving Size

Makes 16 pieces

Nutritional Facts (Values per Serving)

Calories/serving: 64

Total Carbohydrate: 7 g

Cholesterol: 1 mg

Total Fat: 4 g

Ingredients

Ground pepper – A pinch

Honey – Half tsp

Apricots – 16

Blue cheese (crumbled) – 8 tsp

Pistachios (chopped) – 2 ounces

Preparation Method

1. Slice all the apricots in half.

2. Put half spoon cheese over each and drizzle the cheese with honey.

3. Garnish with pepper and pistachios and serve!

Mousse With Liver and Chicken

Serving Size

Makes 3 cups

Nutritional Facts (Values per Serving)

Calories/serving: 102

Total Carbohydrate: 6 g

Cholesterol: 130 mg

Total Fat: 4 g

Ingredients

Thyme (chopped) – 1 tsp

Brandy – Quarter cup

Sage leaves – 10

Garlic cloves (peeled) – 2

Tart apple – 1

Shallots (chopped) – Half cup

Onions – 1 lb

Nutmeg (grated) – Quarter tsp

Ground pepper – 1 tsp

Salt – 1 tsp

Chicken livers – 1 lb

Extra virgin olive oil – 2 Tbsp

Preparation Method

1. Heat some oil in a pan and put chicken liver in it. Add salt, pepper and a pinch of nutmeg in the pan too. Keep the pan on medium heat until the chicken liver turns brown. Make sure every side of the chicken liver is properly cooked.

2. Take it out in a bowl, cover it with a lid and refrigerate it.

3. Now put shallots, onions and garlic to the pan and stir them while the pan is on the stove. Sprinkle some salt and pepper over the vegetables and then include sage, brandy, thyme and apple too while constantly stirring the contents.

4. When all the ingredients turn soft, take them out in a bowl and refrigerate this bowl too for a while.

5. Now put the cooled liver and vegetable sin the food processor and pulse them until they are properly mixed. Take the mixture out in a bowl and stir it to evenly mix all the ingredients.

6. Cover the bowl with a plastic wrap and keep it in the refrigerator for almost an hour.

7. Take it out and serve!

Spicy Mississippian Pecans

Serving Size

Makes 4 cups

Nutritional Facts (Values per Serving)

Calories/serving: 107

Total Carbohydrate: 11 g

Total Fat: 2 g

Ingredients

Extra virgin olive oil – 2 tbsp

Pimento d'Espelette – Half tsp

Ground pepper – Half tsp

Rosemary – 1 tsp

Thyme (chopped) – 1 tsp

Kosher salt – One and a Half tsp

Dark brown sugar – 1 tbsp

Pecan – 1 lb

Preparation Method

1. Heat the oven at 350 Fahrenheit.

2. Slice the pecans into half and spread them on baking pan. Keep them in the oven for about 12 minutes.

3. Take rest of the ingredients and mix them in a bowl. Top the bowl ingredients with the spice mixture and mix them once again.

4. You can serve this appetizer warm or after refrigerating. Your choice!

Spread with Ham

Serving Size

Makes 2 cups

Nutritional Facts (Values per Serving)

Calories/serving: 72

Total Carbohydrate: 3 g

Cholesterol: 18 mg

Total Fat: 3 g

Ingredients

Parsley – Quarter cup

Cream cheese (low fat) – 8 ounces

Sherry vinegar – 1 Tbsp

Paprika (smoked) – Half tsp

Red peppers – 1 cup

Ham (diced) – One and a half cup

Preparation Method

1. Put all the ingredients in the food processor except cream cheese and pulse them. Make sure that ham has turned into fine pieces.

2. Add cream cheese and run the processor again.

3. Take them out in a bowl and serve

Scandinavian Treats

Serving Size

Makes 40 pieces

Nutritional Facts (Values per Serving)

Calories/serving: 18

Total Carbohydrate: 2 g

Cholesterol: 1 mg

Total Fat: 1 g

Ingredients

Ground pepper – Half tsp

Salt – 1 tsp

Fresh dill – For garnishing

Red onion (chopped) – 2 Tbsp

Sour cream (reduced fat) – 2 Tbsp

Red potatoes – 6

Herring fillets – 18 ounces

Preparation Method

1. Boil the potatoes until they are tender and after they cool off, peel the skin and slice them into half. Sprinkle salt on the potatoes.

2. Slice herring fillets into small pieces as well. They should be small enough to fit in the potato slices.

3. Place a small herring piece on every potato slice. Pour sour cream on the potato and herring fillet and garnish it with red onion, pepper and dill. Serve!

Special Thanksgiving Sauce

Serving Size

Makes about 3 cups sauce

Nutritional Facts (Values per Serving)

Calories/serving: 605

Total Carbohydrate: 129 g

Cholesterol: 0 mg

Total Fat: 0.1 g

Ingredients

Port wine 1 cup

Cornstarch - 1 ½ Tbsp

Cranberries – 3 cups

Cold water – ¼ cup

Sugar – 1 ½ cup

Preparation Method

1. Put berries, sugar and wine in a saucepan. Bring it to boil.

2. Cook for 6 – 7 minutes.

3. Dissolve cornstarch in cold water.

4. Mix the cornflower water in the saucepan.

5. Bring it to boil.

6. Special thanksgiving sauce is ready to serve with any chicken and turkey dish.

Berrylicious Sauce

Serving Size

Makes about 5 cups sauce

Nutritional Facts (Values per Serving)

Calories/serving: 175

Total Carbohydrate: 45.2 g

Cholesterol: 0 mg

Total Fat: 0.1 g

Ingredients

Frozen raspberries – 1 cup

Fresh cranberries – 12 oz.

Grand Marnier – 2 Tbsp (Substitute: Orange Juice)

Sugar – 1 cup

Preparation Method

1. Set the oven to preheat at 350oF.

2. Line the cranberries in a baking pan.

3. Add sugar in it mix well.

4. Put it in the preheated oven for 40 – 45 minutes. Stir once in between.

5. Add in it the frozen raspberries and Grand Marnier. Mix well.

6. Let it cool for a while before serving.

Green Meat Soup with Toast

Serving Size

Serves 4

Nutritional Facts (Values per Serving)

Calories/serving: 495.2

Total Carbohydrate: 41.7 g

Cholesterol: 33 mg

Total Fat: 24.4 g

Ingredients

Chicken broth – 14 oz.

French bread slices – 4

Italian sausage, casings removed and crumbled – ½ lb.

Vermicelli – half cup

Parmesan cheese, grated – 2 tsp.

Garlic, chopped – 1 Tbsp

Fresh spinach, stems shortened – 1 lb.

Water – 2 cups

Extra virgin olive oil – 4 tsp

Preparation Method

7. In a large saucepot, add Italian sausage and cook for 5 minutes while stirring occasionally.

8. Add chopped garlic in it and cook for another minutes.

9. Add chicken broth, spinach and water.

10. Cover and bring it to a boil.

11. Add vermicelli in pot.

12. Cover and boil for 2 more minutes. Set aside.

13. Heat a broiler.

14. Broil the French bread slices on a cookie sheet. Broil for seconds per side.

15. On each slice, sprinkle half teaspoon parmesan cheese and 1 teaspoon oil.

16. Serve the slices with soup.

Quick and Light Meatball Soup

Serving Size

Serves 4

Nutritional Facts (Values per Serving)

Calories/serving: 75.4

Total Carbohydrate: 12.5 g

Cholesterol: 1.1 mg

Total Fat: 0.8 g

Ingredients

Chicken broth – 12 oz.

Italian seasoning, crushed – ½ tsp

Frozen Italian style cooked meatballs – 8 oz.

Italian style stewed tomatoes – 12 oz.

Frozen mixed vegetables – 1 cup

Water -1 ½ cups

Parmesan cheese, grated – 1 Tbsp.

Small dry pasta – Half cup

Preparation Method

1. In a saucepot, add chicken broth, Italian style stewed tomatoes, Italian seasoning and water. Bring it to a boil.

2. Add in it, meatballs, mixed vegetables and pasta. Bring it to a boil.

3. Reduce the heat, cover the pot and let it simmer for 10 minutes.

4. Take it out in a serving bowl and garnish with grated cheese.

Fall Special – Bean Soup

Serving Size

Serves 4

Nutritional Facts (Values per Serving)

Calories/serving: 331.1

Total Carbohydrate: 41 g

Cholesterol: 0.0 mg

Total Fat: 12 g

Ingredients

Canned black beans – 14 oz.

Onion, diced – 1 medium sized

Olive oil – 3 Tbsp.

Garlic cloves – 3

Ground cumin – 1 Tbsp.

Vegetable broth – 2 cups

Cilantro, chopped – ¼ cup

Salt and pepper to taste

Preparation Method

1. Heat olive oil in a saucepot over medium heat.

2. Sauté onions in it till the onions become translucent.

3. Add ground cumin and stir for 30 seconds.

4. Now add garlic and cook for another minute.

5. Add half of the black beans and vegetable broth in it.

6. Bring it to a simmer while stirring occasionally.

7. Turn off the heat.

8. Blend the ingredients in the saucepot using an electric blender.

9. Add all the remaining ingredients and beans in the pot. Blend well.

10. Flame the stove again and bring the blended mixture to a simmer.

11. Take it out in a serving bowl and garnish with chopped cilantro.

Chicken Tortilla Stew

Serving Size

Serves 4 – 5

Nutritional Facts (Values per Serving)

Calories/serving: 924

Total Carbohydrate: 83.9 g

Cholesterol: 88 mg

Total Fat: 47.8 g

Ingredients

Chicken breasts, skinless, thinly sliced – 2 breasts

Tortilla chips – 16 oz.

Canned diced tomatoes – 14 oz.

Olive oil – 2 Tbsp

Avocado, chopped – 2

Chicken broth – 4 cups

Cumin – 2 tsp

Onion, diced – 1 small sized

Fresh cilantro, chopped – 2/3 cup

Carrots, thinly sliced - 2

Monterey jack cheese, grated – half cup

Chili powder – ½ Tbsp

Cayenne pepper – ¼ tsp

Garlic cloves, crushes – 3

Bay leaf – 2

Salt – ½ tsp

Pepper to taste

Preparation Method

1. Heat olive oil over high heat in a large saucepot.

2. Add onion, half of the chopped cilantro and garlic in the pot. Sauté for 2 – 3 minutes.

3. Add diced tomatoes and spices in the pot. Bring it to a boil.

4. Now add in it, chicken slices, carrots and broth.

5. Bring it to a boil. Reduce heat to medium and cook for about 12 minutes.

6. Add half of the cheese and about a cup tortilla chips in the pot. Stir for a minute.

7. Take it out in a serving bowl.

8. Garnish with remaining cilantro, cheese, tortilla chips and avocado.

Thanksgiving Salads and Sidelines

Pink Salad with Cranberries

Serving Size

Serves 24 people

Nutritional Facts (Values per Serving)

Calories/serving: 182

Total Carbohydrate: 22.4 g

Cholesterol: 270.1 mg

Total Fat: 10.7 g

Ingredients

Water – Quarter cup

Sugar – 1 cup + 6 Tbsp

Cranberries – 2 cups

Pecans – 1 cup

Bananas (chopped) – 3

Whipped cream – 1 pint

Fruit cocktail (light syrup) – 28 ounces

Preparation Method

1. You need to boil the cranberries a day before you have to serve.

2. Now take out the boiled cranberries in a bowl, mesh them and mix them with sugar, and chopped nuts.

3. Cover the bowl with a lid and refrigerate it overnight.

4. Take the bowl out before serving and include fruit cocktail, whipped cream, vanilla and sugar in it. Mix all the ingredients well.

5. Take banana, mesh it and put it in the bowl too.

6. Mix and serve cold!

Onions with Creamed Peas

Serving Size

Serves 3 people

Nutritional Facts (Values per Serving)

Calories/serving: 326.6

Total Carbohydrate: 53 g

Cholesterol: 4 mg

Total Fat: 5.7 g

Ingredients

Margarine – 1 Tbsp

Cornstarch – 1 Tbsp

Milk (low fat) – 1 cup

White pearl onions – One and a half cup

English peas – One and a half lb

Salt – Quarter tsp

Ground pepper – Quarter tsp

Preparation Method

1. Wash the peas and remove onion's skin. Boil these both vegetables and make sure that they turn soft.

2. Drain the water and take out the vegetables in a bowl.

3. Put the rest of the ingredients in a sauce pan and bring them to boil.

4. After boiling the milk will turn thick and when it does, add onions and peas to the sauce pan.

5. Serve!

Onions and Spinach Salad

Serving Size

Serves 6 people

Nutritional Facts (Values per Serving)

Calories/serving: 777.9

Total Carbohydrate: 58.1 g

Cholesterol: 96.1 mg

Total Fat: 60.1 g

Ingredients

Oranges – 1 can

Bean sprouts – 1 can

Water chestnuts – 1 can

Spinach – 2 bags

Slivered almonds – Half cup

Bacon (sliced) – 11 slices

Eggs – 2

Worcestershire sauce – 1 tsp

Catsup – Quarter dup

Brown sugar – 3 quarter cup

Cider vinegar – 3 Tbsp

Yellow onion – 1

Canola oil – 1 cup

Preparation Method

1. Boil the eggs from 10 to 12 minutes and when they cool off, remove their skin and chop them.

2. On the other hand fry the bacon and split it into small pieces.

3. Next, toast the almonds until they turn golden brown.

4. Put greens in a bowl and keep them on the side.

5. Rinse oranges, sprouts and chestnuts with sink sprayer and let the liquid dry out.

6. Now put Worcestershire sauce, catsup, brown sugar, cider vinegar, yellow onion and canola oil in the food processor and pulse them until they all turn into fine pieces.

7. Include sprouts, oranges, water and chestnuts in the bowl with the greens and mix well.

8. Stop the bowl ingredients with the food processor's ingredients.

9. Serve the salad!

Garlic-Y Mashed Potatoes

Serving Size

Serves 8 people

Nutritional Facts (Values per Serving)

Calories/serving: 408.9

Total Carbohydrate: 37.2 g

Cholesterol: 77.2 mg

Total Fat: 27.3 g

Ingredients

Paprika – For garnishing

Chives (chopped) – For garnishing

Butter – Half cup

Cream cheese – 8 ounces

Sour cream – 8 ounces

Garlic cloves – 8

Yukon gold potatoes – 10

Preparation Method

1. Slice the potatoes in quarters, with the skin on and boil them.

2. Include garlic cloves in the boiled water too.

3. When these both ingredients turn soft, drain the water.

4. Include butter, sour cream and cream cheese in the pot too and mesh them all in a potato masher.

5. Pour the mixture in an oven proof dish and sprinkle chives and paprika over the ingredients.

6. Keep the dish in the oven and bake it for 15 to 20 minutes.

7. Take it out and serve!

Simple Salad with Pearl Onions

Serving Size

Serves 4 people

Nutritional Facts (Values per Serving)

Calories/serving: 156.9

Total Carbohydrate: 19.9 g

Cholesterol: 22.9 mg

Total Fat: 8.7 g

Ingredients

Parsley (chopped) – 2 Tbsp

Pepper – Quarter tsp

Dijon mustard – 1 tsp

Light brown sugar – 3 Tbsp

Pearl onions (frozen) – 1 lb

Butter – 3 tbsp

Salt – Quarter tsp

Preparation Method

1. Take a frying pan and melt some butter in it.

2. When it turns in liquid form, add sliced onion in it and keep it on the stove until the onion turns brown.

3. Add mustard, brown sugar, parsley, salt and pepper in the pan and keep stirring all the while.

4. Take it out in a serving bowl and garnish it with chopped parsley before serving.

Turnip Salad

Serving Size

Serves 6 people

Nutritional Facts (Values per Serving)

Calories/serving: 187.1

Total Carbohydrate: 20.3 g

Cholesterol: 89.3 mg

Total Fat: 9.9 g

Ingredients

Butter – 2 Tbsp

Breadcrumbs – Half cup

Nutmeg – A pinch

Baking powder – 1 tsp

Brown sugar – 1 Tbsp

Flour – 3 Tbsp

Eggs – 2

Butter – 2 Tbsp

Turnips (cubed) – 6 cups

Salt – A pinch

Ground pepper – A pinch

Preparation Method

1. Take a pan and cook turnips in it until they turn soft.

2. Include eggs and butter in the pan too.

3. Mix sugar, flour, seasoning, baking powder and nutmeg in a bowl and mix them well before pouring them in the pan.

4. Stir the pan mixture.

5. Take it out in a casserole dish and sprinkle some breadcrumbs on the top.

6. Keep the dish in the oven and let it bake for approximately 25 minutes. Take it out and serve!

Spicy Green Salad

Serving Size

Serves 6 people

Nutritional Facts (Values per Serving)

Calories/serving: 123.4

Total Carbohydrate: 4 g

Cholesterol: 0 mg

Total Fat: 12.1 g

Ingredients

Kosher salt – A pinch

Paprika – 1 tsp

Almonds (sliced) – 3 quarter cup

Red grapes (seedless0 – 3 quarter cup

Parsley – Quarter cup

Red radishes – 6

Mixed greens – 3 cups

Extra virgin olive oil – Quarter cup

Red wine vinegar – 1 Tbsp

Grainy mustard – 2 tsp

Salt – Quarter tsp

Preparation Method

1. Heat the oven before hand at 350 Fahrenheit.

2. Put almonds, salt and paprika in the blender and make sure that it turns into fine pieces.

3. Take almonds out on a baking pan and keep them in the oven for almost 5 minutes.

4. Take a bowl and mix red wine vinegar, a pinch of salt, and mustard in it and keep the bowl aside.

5. Slice the radishes and then mix them with parsley, grapes and greens. Put all of these ingredients in the blender and run it until it is finely chopped.

6. Take them out in a bowl, top it with almonds and other bowl ingredients and serve!

Mashed Potatoes

Serving Size

Serves 11 people

Nutritional Facts (Values per Serving)

Calories/serving: 206.8

Total Carbohydrate: 33.3 g

Cholesterol: 22.9 mg

Total Fat: 11.5 g

Ingredients

Paprika – Halt tsp

Butter 0 1 Tbsp

Milk – Quarter

Sour cream – Half cup

Cream cheese – 2 packets

Potatoes – 3 lbs

Salt – Half tsp

Preparation Method

1. Boil the potatoes in salted water.

2. When they turn soft, drain the water.

3. Include butter, milk, sour cream and cream cheese in the pot too and mesh them all in a potato masher.

4. Pour the mixture in an oven proof dish and sprinkle paprika over the ingredients.

5. Keep the dish in the oven and bake it for 15 to 20 minutes.

6. Take it out and serve!

Cranberry and Walnut Stuffing

Serving Size

Serves 4 people

Nutritional Facts (Values per Serving)

Calories/serving: 266.1

Total Carbohydrate: 25.4 g

Cholesterol: 1.2 mg

Total Fat: 16.4 g

Ingredients

Chicken flavored stuffing mix – 1 package

Water – 1 cup

Butter – 2 Tbsp

Cranberries (dried) – half cup

Walnuts (toasted) – Half cup

Preparation Method

1. Take a sauce pan and put water along with butter and cranberries in it. Keep it on high heat until the water boils.

2. Include the stuffing mix in the pan too and stir.

3. Remove the pan from the stove and after 5 minutes add walnuts too.

4. Take it out in a serving dish, garnish with fresh parsley and serve!

Thanksgiving Lunch

Healthy Bean Casserole

Serving Size

Serves 8

Nutritional Facts (Values per Serving)

Calories/serving: 144

Total Carbohydrate: 15.6 g

Cholesterol: 1 mg

Total Fat: 7.6 g

Ingredients

Cream of mushroom soup – 1 can

Milk - Half cup

Frozen green cut beans- 2 packages

Diced pimento pepper – 1 jar, drained

French-fried onions – 1 can

Water – 1 cup

Ground black pepper - 1/8 tsp

Preparation Method

1. Set the oven to 175 degrees C for preheating for fifteen minutes.

2. Submerge the beans in boiling water in a medium sized pan. Bring to boil over medium heat. Once boiled, cover and let cook for 5 minutes. Once tender, remove from heat and drain the beans.

3. Take a square 8 inch dish and lightly butter it.

4. In a separate bowl, mix the rest of the ingredients except the onions and spread it in the square glass dish. Sprinkle the onions on the top of the mixture on the dish.

5. Place the dish in the oven and bake uncovered for 30 minutes until the casserole is bubbly in the centre.

6. The dish is ready to be served.

Roasted Thanksgiving Turkey

Serving Size

Serves 12

Nutritional Facts (Values per Serving)

Calories/serving: 796.2

Total Carbohydrate: 16.0 g

Cholesterol: 308.7 mg

Total Fat: 36.7 g

Ingredients for Turkey

Coarsely chopped celery - 1 bunch

Chopped carrots - 4

Chopped onions - 4

White portion of 2 leeks chopped

Sliced orange - 1

Dried basil - 2 Tbsp

Turkey – 12 pounds

Ingredients for Glaze

White wine -4 oz

Apple juice concentrate – 4 oz

Orange juice – 6 oz

Lemon juice – 2 oz

Soy sauce – 2 Tbsp

Preparation Method

1. Preheat the oven at 400 degrees.

2. Take a roasting pan big enough to place the turkey but don't place it in the pan yet.

3. In this roasting pan, add celery, carrots and onions.

4. Take a small bowl and add orange, leek, and the basil in it.

5. Place this mixture in the cavity created in the turkey after cleaning it.

6. Take the stuffed turkey and place it on the roasting pan in which you earlier placed the vegetables.

7. Next you will have to make glaze by combining all the ingredients for glaze together.

8. Place the pan in the oven for half hour. After the half hour is over, baste the turkey with the glaze and lower the temperature to 350 degrees. Cook it for a further 2 hours.

9. Keep basting the turkey with glaze after every fifteen minutes during the cooking time.

10. After the turkey is done, let it cool for an approximate 20 minutes.

11. After the juices have drained off the turkey, pour them off the pan into a bowl to use as gravy with the turkey. You must pour off the fat first before using the gravy.

12. Taste to check if the seasoning needs to be adjusted in the gravy. Add salt and pepper if it does.

13. The turkey is ready for carving.

Warm Delicate Pear

Serving Size

Serves 3

Nutritional Facts (Values per Serving)

Calories/serving: 241

Total Carbohydrate: 43 g

Cholesterol: 0 mg

Total Fat: 0 g

Ingredients

Ripe pears - 4

Fruity white wine – 2 cups

Honey - ¼ Cup

Cinnamon sticks - 5

Bay leaves - 5

Orange zest – 3 strips

Preparation Method

1. 15 minutes prior to baking, Preheat the oven to 400°F

2. Make the pears stand on a plate by leveling them from the bottom. Arrange them in a baking dish after leveling.

3. Mix the rest of the ingredients and pour over the pears.

4. Bake the pears for 1 hour and at fifteen minutes intervals, baste the pears with the syrup surrounding it.

5. When wrinkled, they are done. Using a slotted spoon transfer the pears to a serving dish.

6. Pour the wine mixture into a saucepan and boil till thickened and sauce like consistency. Pour over the pears and serve.

Turkey Stuffing

Serving Size

Serves 10

Nutritional Facts (Values per Serving)

Calories/serving: 183

Total Carbohydrate: 26 g

Cholesterol: 17 mg

Total Fat: 4 g

Ingredients

Whole wheat bread cubed - 12 slices

Turkey sausage – 8 oz

Oil – 2 Tblsp

Chopped celery – 3 stalks

Chopped Onions – 2 mediums

Chopped Garlic – 1 clove

Peeled and chopped apples - 3

Chopped fresh or dried Sage - 2 tsp

Fresh or dry thyme – 1/2 tsp

Dried basil 2 tsp

Chicken broth – 2 cups

Salt – 1/4 tsp

Pepper to taste

Preparation Method

1. Preheat oven at 350°F.

2. For toasting the bread, we have to spread it on a baking sheet and lightly bake. This should take up to 15 to 20 minutes.

3. While the break is baking, fry the sausage in a non stick pan stirring it to break it apart. Cook till 10 minutes until no longer pink. Drain and keep aside.

4. Now add oil to the pan and add celery, onions and garlic and cook till soft. Then add apples and cook for a further 10 minutes. Set the mixture aside in a large bowl.

5. Combine the vegetables and apple mixture with toasted bread, sausage and the herbs. Add the broth to the mixture also. Add salt and pepper.

6. Spread the mixture to a baking pan and cover the pan with baking foil. Bake for 45 minutes.

Sweet Potatoes Delight

Serving Size

Serves 10

Nutritional Facts (Values per Serving)

Calories/serving: 242

Total Carbohydrate: 36 g

Cholesterol: 46 mg

Total Fat: 10 g

Ingredients for Potatoes

Sweet potatoes - 2 1/2 pounds chopped into bite size

Eggs - 2

Oil – 1 Tbsp

Honey – 1 Tbsp

Milk – Half cup

Orange zest – 2 tsp

Vanilla extract – 2 tsp

Salt – 1/2 tsp

Ingredients for Topping

Whole wheat flour– Half cup

Brown sugar- 1/3 cup

Frozen orange juice concentrate – 4 tsp

Oil – 1 Tbsp

Butter – 1 Tbsp

Pecans - 1/2 cup chopped

Preparation Method

1. Preheat oven to 350°F.

2. Boil sweet potatoes till soft

3. Mash after removing skin

4. Prepare a square 8 inch baking dish by buttering it.

5. In a bowl whisk eggs, honey and oil and add mashed potatoes to this mixture.

6. Now add milk, vanilla, orange and salt to the mixture and mix well.

7. Spoon the mixture in to the prepared dish and level it using a tablespoon.

8. Now prepare topping by mixing all the topping ingredients except pecans. Once mixed it should have a crumbly consistency.

9. Stir in pecans and spread over the potato mixture in the glass dish.

10. Bake the dish and its contents for 35 minutes. It should be browned on the top.

11. Serve.

Sugar, Spice and Everything Nice Turkey

Serving Size

Serves 10

Nutritional Facts (Values per Serving)

Calories/serving: 850

Total Carbohydrate: 26.0 g

Cholesterol: 150.7 mg

Total Fat: 39.7 g

Ingredients

Whole turkey – 12 pounds

Light brown sugar – 1/4 Cup

Salt – 2 Tbsp

Onion powder – 1tsp

Garlic powder – 1/2 tsp

Ground allspice – 1/2 tsp

Ground cloves – 1/2 tsp

Ground mace – 1/2 tsp

Onion - 1

Chicken broth – 2 cans

Flour – 2 Tbsp

Preparation Method

1. Clean, rinse and dry turkey. Take a string and tie the two legs together and tuck the wings under. Mix brown sugar and all the spices and rub over turkey. Cover and chill the marinated turkey for the next 8 hours.

2. Take a roasting pan and place the turkey breast side up on the pan.

3. Arrange the onions on the side of the turkey, inside the pan and pour the broth on top of the onions.

4. For the next 1 ½ hours, bake this turkey at 325 degrees, loosely covered.

5. Remove the cover and bake for an additional 1 ½ hours.

6. Remove the turkey and let cool for 20 minutes before carving.

7. Reserve the pan drippings, de-fat it and discard the onions.

8. Pour the drippings in a sauce pan and combine it with flour, mixing to dissolve lumps. Boil until thickened and serve with turkey.

Lemonized Green Beans

Serving Size

Serves 4

Nutritional Facts (Values per Serving)

Calories/serving: 74

Total Carbohydrate: 10 g

Cholesterol: 0 mg

Total Fat: 4 g

Ingredients

Trimmed green beans – 1 pound

Chopped fresh dill – 4 tsp

Minced shallot – 4 tsp

Olive oil – 1 Tbsp

Lemon juice – 1 Tbsp

Mustard – 1 tsp

Salt – ¼ tsp

Pepper to taste

Preparation Method

1. Steam the beans by placing in a steamer until crisp, for 5 to 7 minutes. Drain and set aside.

2. Whisk together the rest of the ingredients in a large bowl and toss the beans in it to coat.

3. Serve after ten minutes.

Herbilicious Turkey

Serving Size

Serves 10

Nutritional Facts (Values per Serving)

Calories/serving: 264

Total Carbohydrate: 1.7 g

Cholesterol: 142 mg

Total Fat: 4.9 g

Ingredients

Whole turkey – 12 pounds

Chopped fresh sage – 2 Tbsp

Chopped chives – 3 tsp

Chopped thyme – 2 tsp

Chopped parsley – 2 tsp

Chicken broth – 3 cups

Dry sherry - 1/3 cup

Flour – 2Tbsp

Preparation Method

1. Preheat oven to 350 degrees.

2. Clean, rinse and dry turkey. Take a string and tie the two legs together and tuck the wings under. Combine sage, chives, thyme, parsley and rub inside the turkey's cavity.

3. Take a roasting pan and place the turkey breast side up on the pan.

4. For the next 1 ½ hours, bake this turkey at 325 degrees, loosely covered.

5. Remove the cover and bake for an additional 1 ½ hours.

6. Remove the turkey and let cool for 20 minutes before carving.

7. Pour the drippings in a sauce pan, pour the fat off it or use a de-fat bowl to separate the fat from the drippings.

8. Stir in the saucepan the broth (reserve ¼ cup of broth from this) and sherry and boil till thickened.

9. Take 1/4 cup from broth and add flour to it and mix. Mix in the sherry and broth mixture prepared in the previous step. Add in the 2 tablespoons parsley, 1 teaspoon of chives and thyme and serve this sauce with turkey.

Thanksgiving Cheese Balls

Serving Size

Makes 4 dozen balls

Nutritional Facts (Values per Serving)

Calories/serving: 64

Total Carbohydrate: 1 g

Cholesterol: 11 mg

Total Fat: 6 g

Ingredients

Pecans (toasted and chopped) – One and a half cups

Garlic powder – Half tsp

Onion (grated) – 1 tsp

Pimientos (chopped) – 3 Tbsp

Mayonnaise (low fat) – 3 Tbsp

Monterey jack cheese (shredded) – 2 cups

Cheddar cheese (shredded) – 2 cups

Cream cheese (reduced fat) – Quarter cup

Salt and pepper – A pinch

Preparation Method

1. Put all the cheeses in the food processor and run the machine until all of them mix properly.

2. Slowly start adding rest of the ingredients too, one by one, except the pecans. Making sure that all of them are pulsed and mixed properly.

3. Now take out pecans in a bowl and form small sized balls with the mixture of the food processor. Roll the bowls in the bowl with the pecans.

4. Your cheese balls are done! You can serve them at the time or after refrigerating them for a while, your choice!

Crusted Red Onions and Pears

Serving Size

Serves 8 people

Nutritional Facts (Values per Serving)

Calories/serving: 188

Total Carbohydrate: 29 g

Cholesterol: 3 mg

Total Fat: 7 g

Ingredients

Parmigiano-Reggiano (grated) – Quarter cup

Breadcrumbs (dry) – 1 cup

Salt – Quarter tsp

Thyme (chopped) – 1 Tbsp

Extra virgin olive oil – 3 Tbsp

Pears – 3

Red onion – 1

Pepper – A pinch

Preparation Method

1. First set the oven at 400 Fahrenheit. Next take a large bowl and fill it with water. Slice onion into wedges and immerse them in water while placing them in a sieve. Let the onion wedges stay in water for about 20 minutes.

2. After that you need to slice each pear into 16 pieces. Drain water from the onion and take out the wedges and place them along the pear slices.

3. Put them in the baking dish and top it with a tablespoon of oil, salt, pepper and thyme. Cover the baking dish with foil.

4. Keep it in the oven for about half an hour.

5. While onions and peas are roasting, mix breadcrumbs and cheese in another bowl. Pour two tablespoons of oil on the mixture and stir it to mix properly.

6. Take out the baking pan from the oven and top it with cheese and breadcrumbs mixture. Keep it back in the oven and let it roast until the breadcrumbs turn brown. That will take about 15 to minutes.

7. Take it out, transfer it in a serving dish and enjoy!

Roasted Tomatoes with Baked Ziti

Serving Size

> Serves 6 people

Nutritional Facts (Values per Serving)

> Calories/serving: 241.7
>
> Total Carbohydrate: 39.1 g
>
> Cholesterol: 23.4 mg
>
> Total Fat: 2.8 g

Ingredients

> Mozzarella cheese (low fat) – 3 quarter cup
>
> Ziti pasta (cooked) – 8 ounces
>
> Oregano leaves (chopped) – 2 tsp
>
> Tomatoes (diced0 – 1 can
>
> Tomato sauce – 1 can
>
> Zucchini (sliced lengthwise) – 1
>
> Garlic cloves – 2
>
> Sweet onion (chopped) – 1 cup
>
> Lean ground beef – Half lb
>
> Pepper – Quarter tsp
>
> Salt – Quarter tsp
>
> Cooking spray

Preparation Method

1. First, heat the oven at 375 Fahrenheit and then coat the baking dish with cooking spray.

2. Now take a cooking pan and put onion, garlic and beef in it. Keep the pan on medium heat and let the ingredients cook for a while.

3. Add diced tomatoes, salt, pepper, oregano and tomato sauce in the pan too. Stir the ingredients well.

4. Transfer the pan ingredients in the baking dish along with the pasta and top it with cheese.

5. Cover the baking dish with a foil and keep it in the oven.

6. After 15 minutes, take it out and serve!

Thanksgiving-Y Tortellini

Serving Size

Serves 2 people

Nutritional Facts (Values per Serving)

Calories/serving: 1137.3

Total Carbohydrate: 92.6 g

Cholesterol: 276 mg

Total Fat: 71.6 g

Ingredients

Baby peas (frozen) – 3 quarter cup

Parmesan cheese (grated) – Quarter cup

Nutmeg (grated) – 1 pinch

Heavy cream – 1 cup

Prosciutto (sliced) – Quarter lb

Garlic cloves – 2

Butter – 2 Tbsp

Water – Quarter cup

Cheese tortellini – 12 ounces

Salt and pepper – A pinch

Preparation Method

1. First of all cook tortellini following the instructions mentioned on the packet.

2. Now take out a pan and melt some butter in it. Then include the garlic cloves in the pan.

3. Include prosciutto, nutmeg, peas and parmesan in the pan and cook for about 2 minutes. Next add heavy cream in the pan and let the ingredients boil.

4. You will see that the cream has thickened. When it does, add tortellini in the pan along with salt and pepper.

5. Mix the ingredients well, take it out and enjoy!

Turkey gravy

Serving Size

Serves 5 people

Nutritional Facts (Values per Serving)

Calories/serving: 225.2

Total Carbohydrate: 13.1 g

Cholesterol: 48.8 mg

Total Fat: 18.5 g

Ingredients

Black pepper – Half tsp

All purpose flour – Half cup + 3 Tbsp

Butter – Half cup

Chicken broth – 4 cups

Chicken bouillon broth – 1 Tbsp

Preparation Method

1. Mix chicken bouillon broth and chicken broth in a pan and cook them over low heat.

2. Include lots of black pepper and butter in the pan too and stir the ingredients constantly.

3. Now start adding flour in the pan slowly, stirring all the while to make sure that no solid pieces form in the pan.

4. When the pan mixture starts to thickening and bubbling, remove the pan from the stove and let it cool before serving!

Turkey Adorned With Swiss Panini

Serving Size

Serves 2 people

Nutritional Facts (Values per Serving)

Calories/serving: 741.5

Total Carbohydrate: 90.4g

Cholesterol: 118.6 mg

Total Fat: 26.5 g

Ingredients

Raspberry jam – 2 Tbsp

Baby spinach (trimmed) – 1 bunch

Deli turkey – Half lb

Swiss cheese – 2 slices

Sourdough bread – 4 slices

Butter – 2 Tbsp

Preparation Method

1. Spread butter on one side of the of two bread slices.

2. Now place the buttered slices on the Panini grill with the buttered side facing downwards and put turkey, baby spinach and cheese over the slices.

3. Now spread jam on two slices and place them of the turkey.

4. Cook the sandwiches on the grill for about 5 minutes. You will see that the bread has turned crispy and the cheese has melted.

5. Remove the same process with the rest of the slices.

Dried Turkey with Rosemary

Serving Size

Serves 4 people

Nutritional Facts (Values per Serving)

Calories/serving: 420

Total Carbohydrate: 1.7 g

Cholesterol: 167 mg

Total Fat: 19 g

Ingredients

Juniper berries 9dried) – 3 Tbsp

Thyme (dried0 – 3 Tbsp

Marjoram (dried) – 3 Tbsp

Sea salt – 3 Tbsp

Anise seeds – 2 Tbsp

Black peppercorns – 1 Tbsp

Rosemary sprigs – 12

Garlic cloves – 12

Unsalted butter – Half cup

Turkey – 1

Preparation Method

1. Put salt, thyme, juniper berries, marjoram, anise seeds and peppercorns in the food processor and pulse them until they turn into fine pieces.

2. Next wash the turkey and remove excess fat, neck, wing tips and giblets.

3. Now coat the pulsed mixture all over the turkey and pour some inside the cavity as well.

4. Cover it and keep in the fridge for almost 24 hours.

5. When the turkey is ready for baking, set the oven at 325 Fahrenheit.

6. Take out the turkey and with the help of your washed hands spread it to put garlic and rosemary sprigs in the cavity.

7. Cover the skin of the turkey with butter.

8. Keep it in the oven. Let it roast for at least an hour before flipping it over.

9. Cook the other side for an hour and a half, making sure that it is properly cooked.

10. Take it out, transfer it in a serving dish and enjoy!

Thanksgiving Celebration Cocktails

Martini with Pears

Serving Size

Makes 1 cup

Nutritional Facts (Values per Serving)

Calories/serving: 100

Total Carbohydrate:6 g

Cholesterol: 0 mg

Total Fat: 0 g

Ingredients

Lemon juice – 4 Tbsp

Grapefruit juice – 2 Tbsp

Pear vodka – 2 ounces

Lemon or pear slices

Preparation Method

1. Put all the ingredients in a shaker, add some ice and shake them well.

2. Pour the martini in a glass and garnish it with a pear or lime slice.

Spicy and Gingery Cocktail

Serving Size

Makes 1 cup

Nutritional Facts (Values per Serving)

Calories/serving: 132

Total Carbohydrate: 0 g

Cholesterol: 132 mg

Total Fat: 0 g

Ingredients

Ginger ale

Spiced rum – 2 ounces

Ice

Preparation Method

1. Take a glass, put ice in it and pour spiced rum in it too.

2. Mix it with ginger ale and your cocktail is ready!

Kings Cider

Serving Size

Makes 3 cups

Nutritional Facts (Values per Serving)

Calories/serving: 129.7

Total Carbohydrate: 6.4 g

Cholesterol: 0 mg

Total Fat: 0 g

Ingredients

Cinnamon stick – 1 piece

Cinnamon – 1 dash

Honey – Quarter ounces

Lemon juice – Quarter ounces

Heated cider – 2 ounces

Whiskey – One and a half ounces

Preparation Method

1. Put all the ingredients in a saucepan or a pot, except cinnamon sticks and heat them until they turn mild warm.

2. Take it out in a mug, garnish it with cinnamon stick and devour!

Martini with Caramel Apple Pies

Serving Size

Makes 1 cup

Nutritional Facts (Values per Serving)

Calories/serving: 128.5

Total Carbohydrate: 0 g

Cholesterol: 0 mg

Total Fat: 0 g

Ingredients

Apple Schnapps – 2 Tbsp

Vanilla vodka (iced) – Quarter cup

Cream soda – 1 dash

Dekuyper butterscotch schnapps – 2 Tbsp

Innamon graham cracker (crushed)

Caramel ice cream topping

Preparation Method

1. Pour caramel topping down the sides of the glass.

2. Take out your shaker and put apple Schnapps, vodka, ice and butter shots and shake all the ingredients well.

3. Pour the shacked mixture in the martini glass and add a splash of cream soda. Sprinkle crushed cookies and it's done!

Thanksgiving Margaritas

Serving Size

Makes 1 cup

Nutritional Facts (Values per Serving)

Calories/serving: 190.6

Total Carbohydrate: 16 g

Cholesterol: 130 mg

Total Fat: 4 g

Ingredients

Ginger ale – 6 ounces

Cinnamon schnapps – Half ounce

Rum (apple flavored preferred) – 2 ounces

Preparation Method

1. Pour apple rum in a glass over ice.

2. Add cinnamon schnapps and ginger ale in the apple cider.

3. Stir all the ingredients together and gulp it down!

Cider and Butterscotch

Serving Size

Makes 18 cups

Nutritional Facts (Values per Serving)

Calories/serving: 1.6

Total Carbohydrate: 0.4 g

Cholesterol: 0 mg

Total Fat: 0 g

Ingredients

Cinnamon sticks – 8

Apple cider or apple juice – 1 gallon

Butterscotch schnapps – 2 cups

Preparation Method

1. Take out your slow cooker and put all the ingredients in it.

2. Keep it on low heat for approximately 3 hours.

3. Pour it in glasses with the help of liquid scooper and serve!

Almond-Y Cocktail

Serving Size

Makes 1 cup

Nutritional Facts (Values per Serving)

Calories/serving: 260.9

Total Carbohydrate: 32.2 g

Cholesterol: 17.0 mg

Total Fat: 4.6 g

Ingredients

Milk – 4 ounces

Kahlua – 2 ounces

Amaretto – 2 ounces

Preparation Method

1. Mix all the ingredients in the shaker and pour it over ice in the glass. Enjoy!

Cognac Cosmopolitan

Serving Size

Makes 1 cup

Nutritional Facts (Values per Serving)

Calories/serving: 14.1

Total Carbohydrate: 3.7 g

Cholesterol: 0 mg

Total Fat: 0 g

Ingredients

Cranberry juice – Half ounce

Lemon juice – Half ounces

Cointreau liqueur – Half ounce

Cognac – One and a half ounce

Preparation Method

1. Put all the ingredient in a shaker over ice and shake vigorously.

2. Pour it in a martini glass and garnish it with a lime wedge before serving.

Apple Cinnamon Drink

Serving Size

Makes 4 cups

Nutritional Facts (Values per Serving)

Calories/serving: 12

Total Carbohydrate: 0 g

Cholesterol: 10 mg

Total Fat: 0 g

Ingredients

Apple juice – 3 ounces

Rum (organic) – One and a half ounce

Applejack (organic) – 3 quarter ounces

Ground cinnamon – 1 dash

Cinnamon stick – 1

Preparation Method

1. Put all the ingredients in a shaker over ice and shake them well.

2. Pour it in a martini glass and serve.

Thanksgiving Rum

Serving Size

Makes 1 cup

Nutritional Facts (Values per Serving)

Calories/serving: 146.5

Total Carbohydrate: 11.5 g

Cholesterol: 0 mg

Total Fat: 1.7 g

Ingredients

Cinnamon stick – 1

Whole cloves – 4

Lemon slice – 1

Rum – One and a half ounces

Boiling water – 1 tsp

Honey – 1 tsp

Preparation Method

1. Mix honey with a teaspoon of boiling water.

2. Include cloves, rum and lemon in it.

3. Fill the whole mug with warm water and stir.

4. Garnish it with a cinnamon stick.

Vodka with a Herb-Y Tinge

Serving Size

Makes 1 cup

Nutritional Facts (Values per Serving)

Calories/serving: 69.3

Total Carbohydrate: 0 g

Cholesterol: 0 mg

Total Fat: 0 g

Ingredients

Apple cider – 4 ounces

Vodka (any) – 1 ounce

Galliano (herbal drink) – 2 ounces

Apple slice

Preparation Method

1. Pour all the ingredient in a glass over ice.

2. Garnish it with apple slices and enjoy!

Thanksgiving Dinner

Spicy and Smoky Turkey

Serving Size

Serves 12 people

Nutritional Facts (Values per Serving)

Calories/serving: 744.9

Total Carbohydrate: 4.0 g

Cholesterol: 308.7 mg

Total Fat: 36.7 g

Ingredients

Hickory wood chunks – 6

Ground cinnamon – 1 tsp

Thyme (dried) – 1 tsp

Dry mustard – 2 tsp

Rubber sage (dried) – 2 tsp

Oregano (dried) – 2 tsp

Kosher salt – 1 tsp

Brown sugar – 3 Tbsp

Ground cumin – 2 tsp

Turkey (thawed) – 1 lb

Preparation Method

1. Clean the turkey by removing extra fat and washing it with water.

2. Mix all the ingredients except wood chunks in a bowl to prepare seasoning. Rub it all over the turkey with the help of a cooking brush and make sure the undersides are glazed properly too.

3. Now soak the wood chunks in water for almost an hour.

4. Make the preparations to some turkey by placing the pan in the center of the rack and surrounding it with 25 charcoal briquettes.

5. Put the turkey in a pan, cover it with foil paper and keep it on the grill.

6. Check after a while to make sure that the turkey doesn't burn but don't remove the foil too often or all the smokey effect will wear off.

7. When turkey turns deep brown, take it off the heat.

8. Let it cool for a while, top it with one of our sauces and serve!

Sausage and Apple Stuffing With Wild Rice

Serving Size

Serves 8 people

Nutritional Facts (Values per Serving)

Calories/serving: 102

Total Carbohydrate: 6 g

Cholesterol: 130 mg

Total Fat: 4 g

Ingredients

Parsley – Quarter cup

Pecan pieces (toasted) – Half cup

Italian style pork sausage or turkey – Half lb

Nutmeg – A pinch

Thyme leaves- 1 Tbsp

Garlic cloves (chopped) – 2

Celery leaves – 2 ribs

Cooking apple – 1

Onion – 1

Unsalted butter – 2 Tbsp

Kosher salt – One and a half tsp

Golden Delicious apples (peeled and chopped) – 1

Water – 3 cups

Wild rice – 1 cup

Preparation Method

1. Fill a saucepan with water and add a pinch of salt in it. Keep it on high heat until the water boils and then put rice in it. Reduce the heat and keep

the saucepan on low heat until the rice is tender. That will take about 20 to 30 minutes. When the rice is done, drain the water and keep cooked rice on the side.

2. Now set the oven at 325 Fahrenheit.

3. Take a pan and melt some butter in it. When it turns liquid, include apple, onion, thyme, garlic, celery, mace and a tea spoon of salt and pepper in it.

4. Stir the mixture for a while and when the onion turns golden-brown, add sausage in the pan. Stir it and break it into pieces with the help of a spoon until the sausages change color. That will take about 5 minutes. Make sure that the sausages don't dry out, they should be juicy.

5. Now add pecans, cooked rice and parsley into the pan, all the while stirring.

6. Transfer the pan ingredients into the baking dish, place the lid or cover the dish with an aluminum foil and keep it in the oven.

7. Let the vegetable ad sausage mixture bake for at least half an hour.

8. Take it out; let it cool for a while and the serve!

Brined Turkey

Serving Size

Serves 22 people

Nutritional Facts (Values per Serving)

Calories/serving: 675.7

Total Carbohydrate: 41.3 g

Cholesterol: 216 mg

Total Fat: 27.2 g

Ingredients

Carrot (peeled and sliced) – 1

Onion (peeled and sliced) – 1

Dried thyme leaves – Half cup

Rosemary leaves (dried) – Half cup

Brown sugar – 4 cups

Turkey – 15 lbs

Celery stalk – 1

Butter (unsalted) – 5 Tbsp

Fresh fruit – For garnishing

Salt – 2 cups

Preparation Method

1. First wash the turkey properly with water.

2. Now take a large cooking pan and fill it with water. Add salt, spices and brown sugar in it and make sure that they mix properly.

3. Now put turkey in the cooking pan, making sure that it completely dips in the water. Cover the lid of the cooking pan and place it in the refrigerator. It needs to stay in the fridge for 7 to 8 hours at least.

4. After the given time, remove turkey from the brine solution and drain the solution.

5. Rinse the turkey with plain water once again and make sure that all the salt and sugar particles are removed from the outer and inner skin.

6. In the hollow space of the turkey put celery, carrot and onion and with the help of a cooking brush smear melted butter all over the surface of the turkey.

7. Keep it in a baking dish and put the dish in the oven. Let the turkey roast for 2 or 3 hours.

8. After a while, take out the turkey from the oven and flip it over with the help of a paper towels or oven mitts.

9. Put it back in the oven and let the other side roast. Remember that brined turkey takes less time to cook than the unbrined turkey so keep your eye on the clock.

10. When it is properly cooked, remove it from the oven and let it breathe in the fresh air for 20 minutes or so before carving

11. Take it out in a serving dish and garnish with fresh fruits before serving!

Maple-D Sweet Potatoes

Serving Size

Serves 12 people

Nutritional Facts (Values per Serving)

Calories/serving: 96

Total Carbohydrate: 19 g

Cholesterol: 5 mg

Total Fat: 2 g

Ingredients

Lemon juice – 1 Tbsp

Butter – 2 Tbsp

Maple syrup – Quarter cup

Sweet potatoes (peeled and sliced) – Two and a half lbs

Salt – half tsp

Ground pepper – A pinch

Preparation Method

1. First of all, set the oven at 400 Fahrenheit.

2. Now take out your baking dish and arrange the sliced sweet potties in it.

3. Take a bowl and mix maple syrup, salt, pepper and lemon juice in it. stir it and then pour it over the sweet potatoes arranged in the baking dish.3

4. Cover the dish with aluminum foil and keep in the oven. It will take about 15 minutes to bake.

5. After 15 minutes, remove them from the oven and take them out in a pan. Keep the pan on low heat while stirring constantly. When they start turning brown, remove them from the pan and serve!

Yummilicious Turkey with Apple Cider

Serving Size

Serves 12 people

Nutritional Facts (Values per Serving)

Calories/serving: 338

Total Carbohydrate: 4.5 g

Cholesterol: 138 mg

Total Fat: 11.3 g

Ingredients

Whole allspice (crushed) – 1 Tbsp

Sugar – Quarter cup

Kosher salt – Quarter cup

Apple cider – 8 cups

Black peppercorns – 1 Tbsp

Ginger (peeled and sliced) – 8 slices

Cloves – 6

Bay leaves – 2

Oranges – 2

Butter (unsalted) – 2 Tbsp

Chicken broth (fat free and less sodium) – 1 can

Onion – 1

Parsley sprigs – 4

Thyme – 4

Sage – 4

Garlic cloves – 4

Turkey (frozen or fresh) – 1 lb

Salt – Half tsp

Ground pepper – 1 tsp

Ice

Preparation Method

1. First we need to brine the turkey by filling a cooking pan with water and adding apple cider, salt, sugar, black peppercorns, whole allspice, ginger, and bay leaves and bringing it to boil. Make sure that all the ingredients have dissolved in the water and then turn off the stove and let the solution cool off.

2. Next, rinse the turkey with water and remove neck and giblets from it. Also, remove the extra fat from the turkey.

3. Place orange slices in the cavity of the turkey.

4. Then take a turkey bag and put turkey inside it along with ice and brine solution. Seal the bag and keep it in the refrigerator. You need to refrigerate the turkey for at least 12 hours.

5. After the allotted time, remove turkey form the bad and discard the brine solution, orange slices and the turkey bags.

6. Now wash the turkey with cold water.

7. Take out your baking pan and arrange thyme, onion, parsley, sage and broth in an even layer. Put turkey on the top and coat it with a layer of unsalted butter. Sprinkle some pepper and salt over it and keep it in the oven.

8. Let the turkey roast for at least half an hour.

9. Take it out, flip it over and then keep it back in the oven. After 15 or 20 minutes, remove it from the oven and let it cool off for 20 minutes.

10. Take it out in a serving dish and garnish it with the baked vegetables.

Casseroles with Mixed Vegetables

Serving Size

Serves 8 people

Nutritional Facts (Values per Serving)

Calories/serving: 333.2

Total Carbohydrate: 19.9 g

Cholesterol: 52.9 mg

Total Fat: 26.4 g

Ingredients

Melted butter – Half cup

Cracker crumbs – One and a half cups

Cheddar cheese 9shredded) – 1 cp

Celery (chopped) – 1 cup

Onion – 1 cup

Mixed vegetables (frozen) – 1 package

Preparation Method

1. First prepare the frozen vegetables acceding to the instructions mentioned on the packet.

2. Now take a large bowl and mix cooked vegetables, cheese, onion, celery and mayonnaise in it.

3. Transfer the mixture in a baking pan and coat it with a layer of crackers and butter. Keep the baking pan in the oven and set it at 300 Fahrenheit.

4. Let the casserole bake for at least half an hour. Take it out and serve!

Zesty Turkey

Serving Size

Serves 10 people

Nutritional Facts (Values per Serving)

Calories/serving: 586.7

Total Carbohydrate: 3.1 g

Cholesterol: 221.1 mg

Total Fat: 27.7 g

Ingredients

Cayenne pepper – Quarter tsp

Ground allspice – Quarter tsp

Garlic powder – Half tsp

Ground cumin – 1 tsp

Dried oregano – 1 tsp

Chili powder – 2 tsp

Onion salt – 2 tsp

Chicken broth – 1 can

All purpose flour – 2 Tbsp

Lemon juice – 2 Tbsp

Olive oil – 2 Tbsp

Turkey breast – 1 lb

Preparation Method

1. Prepare the oven by setting it t 350 Fahrenheit and greasing the baking pan with a thin coating of vegetable oil.

2. Coat turkey with a mixture of lime juice and olive oil, making sure that the area under the skin gets properly coated too.

3. Now take a bowl and mix cumin, chili powder, onion salt, dried oregano, cayenne pepper, allspice and garlic powder in it. Coat turkey with some of this mixture too.

4. Keep turkey in the oven for atlatl 2 hours

5. While the turkey is in the oven, prepare the gravy.

6. Take out a saucepan and pour the remaining bowl mixture in it along with the flour and chicken broth.

7. Cook the mixture at low heat while stirring constantly and make sure that everything mixes properly.

8. When the gravy starts turning thick, remove it from the stove.

9. Check on your turkey. If it's done, remove it from the oven, let it cool for a while and serve it with the gravy.

Good Well Roasted Turkey

Serving Size

Serves 16 people

Nutritional Facts (Values per Serving)

Calories/serving: 733.6

Total Carbohydrate: 1.8 g

Cholesterol: 308.7 mg

Total Fat: 36.4 g

Ingredients

Turkey (frozen) – 1 lb

Ginger – Half tsp

Allspice berry – Half Tbsp

Black peppercorns – 1 Tbsp

Vegetable stock – 1 gallon

Brown sugar – Half cup

Kosher salt – 1 cup

Canola oil – A little

Sage leaves – 6

Rosemary sprigs – 4

Cinnamon stick – 1

Onion (sliced) – Half

Red apple – 1

Iced water

Preparation Method

1. First prepare the brine solution by mixing ginger, allspice berry, vegetable stock, black peppercorns, salt and brown sugar in water and boiling the mixture.

2. When it boils, remove it from the stove and let it cool. Then before you start cooking, mix the brine solution with ice water, submerge turkey in it, cover it and refrigerate the turkey.

3. Now take a microwave bowl and mix cinnamon stick, onion and apple in a cup of water and heat it in the microwave for 5 minutes.

4. Take pout the refrigerated turkey from the brine, discard the solution and rinse it with fresh water.

5. Now place turkey on a baking pan and fill its cavity with the microwaved ingredients, sage, and rosemary. Cover it with a thin layer of canola oil and then keep it in the oven.

6. Let it roast for 20 minutes, then take it out and flip the side. When both sides of the turkey are roasted properly, remove it from the oven and wait for 15 minutes before carving and serving.

Sage and Chestnuts with Brussels sprouts

Serving Size

Serves 12 people

Nutritional Facts (Values per Serving)

Calories/serving: 68

Total Carbohydrate: 10 g

Cholesterol: 3 mg

Total Fat: 3 g

Ingredients

Sage (fresh and chopped) – 2 tsp

Chestnuts (chopped) – Quarter cup

Chicken broth – 3 tbsp

Extra virgin olive oil – 1 Tbsp

Butter – 1 Tbsp

Brussels sprouts- 2 lbs

Salt – Half tsp

Ground pepper – Half tsp

Preparation Method

1. Boil some water in a sauce pan and add Brussels sprouts in it. Let them cook for 5 to 8 minutes and when they are soft and tender, turn off the heat. Drain the water.

2. Now take a frying pan and melt some butter and oil in it. Include chestnuts, Brussels sprouts and sage in the pan and don't forget to stir the mixture constantly.

3. Let the vegetable stay on the stove for at least five minutes, sprinkle some salt and pepper over it and mix.

4. Take it out in a serving dish and devour!

Juicy Turkey

Serving Size

Serves 8 people

Nutritional Facts (Values per Serving)

Calories/serving: 1006.8

Total Carbohydrate: 32 g

Cholesterol: 122.1 mg

Total Fat: 101.1 g

Ingredients

Canola oil – Quarter cup

Butter (unsalted) – 4 Tbsp

Apple – 1

Lemon – 1

Sage sprigs – 4

Thyme sprigs – 4

Rosemary sprigs – 4

Turkey (giblets and neck removed) – 1

Turkey bag – 1

Salt – 1 tsp

Ground pepper – A pinch

Preparation Method

5. First, wash the turkey with fresh water.

6. Fill the cavity of the turkey with half lemon, half apple, all herbs and butter. The remaining apple and lemon should be placed in the cavity of the neck.

7. Tie up the turkey with the help of kitchen strings.

8. Cover turkey with a thin layer of canola oil and sprinkle some salt and pepper on the top.

9. Now carefully transfer the turkey in the oven bag along with a tablespoon of water.

10. Keep it in the oven and set it at 350 Fahrenheit.

11. It will take approximately 2 hours to cook. However, make sure you check on it after every 45 minutes.

12. When it's done, take it out and serve!

Turkey Burgers

Serving Size

Serves 4 people

Nutritional Facts (Values per Serving)

Calories/serving: 290.6

Total Carbohydrate: 3.5 g

Cholesterol: 111.6 mg

Total Fat: 18.4 g

Ingredients

Basil leaves (dried) – 1 tsp

Parsley (dried) – 1 tsp

Italian seasoning – 1 tsp

Oregano (dried) – 1 tsp

Olive (chopped) – Half cup

Feta cheese (crumbled) – 1 cup

Garlic powder – Half tsp

Onion powder – 1 tsp

Turkey – 1 lb

Preparation Method

14. Mix all the above mentioned ingredients in a large bowl and make 4 equal patties from the batter.

15. Grill the patties.

16. When they are done, serve them on buns laced with tomato ketchup and garlic mayo.

Turkey Calzone

Serving Size

Serves 4 people

Nutritional Facts (Values per Serving)

Calories/serving: 98.2

Total Carbohydrate: 0.6 g

Cholesterol: 19.3 mg

Total Fat: 7.4 g

Ingredients

Pesto sauce – Quarter cup

Provolone cheese – 4 slices

Pizza dough – 1 can

Turkey breast (sliced) – 16

Preparation Method

1. First set the oven at 44 Fahrenheit.

2. Now spread the pizza dough on a flat surface. Make sure that it flattens evenly and then slice it to from 4 rectangular shapes.

3. Lace each rectangle with pesto sauce, one cheese slice and turkey slices. Wrap the rectangle in half to enclose the filling.

4. Seal the edges of the wrap with the help of the fork.

5. Spread it out on a baking pan and keep it in the oven for about 15 minutes.

6. When they turn brown, take them out and serve!

Delicata With Onions and Squash

Serving Size

Serves 4 people

Nutritional Facts (Values per Serving)

Calories/serving: 164

Total Carbohydrate: 26 g

Cholesterol: 0 mg

Total Fat: 7 g

Ingredients

Dijon mustard – 1 Tbsp

Maple syrup – 1 Tbsp

Rosemary (chopped) – 1 tsp

Extra virgin olive oil – 2 Tbsp

Red onion – 1

Delicata squash – 2 lbs

Salt – Quarter tsp

Preparation Method

1. Heat the oven at 425 Fahrenheit beforehand.

2. Slice squash in half lengthwise and crosswise and remove the seeds. Cut it in thick wedges.

3. Now take out a baking dish, grease it with oil and spread the squash wedges on the baking dish along with a tablespoon of oil, onion rings and salt.

4. Keep it in the oven and let the ingredients bake for half an hour.

5. Prepare the dressing by mixing rosemary, maple syrup and mustard in a bowl.

6. When the baked ingredients turn brown, remove them from the oven and serve with the dressing.

Oven-ized Turkey

Serving Size

Serves 12 people

Nutritional Facts (Values per Serving)

Calories/serving: 686.6

Total Carbohydrate: 3.2 g

Cholesterol: 277.6 mg

Total Fat: 38 g

Ingredients

Garlic (sliced crosswise) – 1

Spanish onion – 1

Lemon - 1

Thyme – 1 bunch

Thyme leaves (chopped) – 1 tsp

Lemon juice – 3 Tbsp

Unsalted butter – Quarter lb

Salt – A pinch

Ground pepper – A pinch

Preparation Method

1. Take a pan and melt butter in it. Add lemon juice and thyme leaves in the pan.

2. Next, wash the turkey with fresh water. Remove any extra fat and place it in a baking pan.

3. Fill the cavity of the turkey with lemon, garlic, onion, thyme sprigs and onion.

4. Cover the skin of the turkey with the melted butter mixture and sprinkle salt and pepper over it.

5. Keep the turkey in the oven and let it roast for almost 2 hours.

6. Take it out in a serving dish, carve and serve!

Crockpot Turkey

Serving Size

Serves 6 people

Nutritional Facts (Values per Serving)

Calories/serving: 747.3

Total Carbohydrate: 3.3 g

Cholesterol: 294.8 mg

Total Fat: 34.1 g

Ingredients

Garlic powder – Half tsp

Olive oil – 1 Tbsp

Turkey breast – 1 whole turkey

Dry onion soup mix – 1 envelope

Ground pepper – Half tsp

Preparation Method

1. Wash the turkey breast and after drying it spread a thin layer of vegetable oil over it.

2. Take a bowl and mix black pepper, garlic and onion soup in it. After mixing it rub it on turkey as well, making sure that it covers every inch of the turkey.

3. Cover it with aluminum foil and refrigerate it for approximately a day.

4. Take it out, remove the foil and cook the turkey in crock pot at low heat for at least 5 to 6 hours.

5. When it's cooked from every side, remove it from the utensil and serve!

Grilly Turkey

Serving Size

Serves 6 people

Nutritional Facts (Values per Serving)

Calories/serving: 8361.2

Total Carbohydrate: 12.6 g

Cholesterol: 3488.4 mg

Total Fat: 411.4 g

Ingredients

Beer – 1 can

Onion (chopped) – 1

Carrot (sliced) – 1

Celery (chopped) – 1

Apple – 1

Turkey – 1 whole

Salt – A pinch

Margarine – 1 bar

Ground pepper – A pinch

Preparation Method

1. Wash the turkey and remove the excess fat.

2. Fill the cavity with vegetables and apple and cover the external skin with margarine. If you are fond of turkey' internal parts, put them around the turkey to enhance the flavor.

3. Next comes the beer. Pour it all over the turkey and make sure that it reaches the internal parts too.

4. Cover the dish with foil and make sure that the foil doesn't touch the turkey.

5. Now place it on the grill and keep it there until it is properly cooked.

Thanksgiving Special Deserts

Marmalade Celebration Cheesecake

Serving Size

Serves 8 – 10

Nutritional Facts (Values per Serving)

Calories/serving: 199

Total Carbohydrate: 26 g

Cholesterol: 30 mg

Total Fat: 7 g

Ingredients

Cottage cheese – 2½ cups

Vanilla snaps – 20 cookies/wafers

Sugar – Half cup

Canola oil – 1 Tbsp

Cornstarch – ¼ cup

Egg whites of 2 eggs

Low fat Cream cheese, 1 inch cubes – 12 oz.

Brown sugar – 1/3 cup

Egg – 1

Fresh orange zest, fresh – 4 tsp

Orange juice – 2 Tbsp

Orange marmalade – 2 Tbsp

Low fat yogurt – 1 cup

Orange juice – 2 Tbsp

Vanilla extract – 1 tsp

Handful of Mint sprigs

Preparation Method

1. Set the oven to preheat at 325°F.

2. Grease a 9 inches springform pan with cooking oil.

3. Wrap the outside of the pan with aluminum foil.

To make the crust,

4. Crush the vanilla snaps in a food processor.

5. Add oil in the processor and continue grinding for a few more minutes.

6. Press the grinded vanilla snaps evenly in the greased springform pan.

To make the filling,

7. Blend the cottage cheese in a food processor. Blend till the cheese becomes a smooth puree.

8. Now add cheese cream, brown sugar, cornstarch and sugar in the processor.

9. Blend for a few more minutes.

10. Add egg, yogurt, egg whites, orange juice, vanilla extract and orange zest in the processor. Blend till it becomes smooth.

11. Pour this puree over the crust in the springform pan.

12. Put the springform pan in a shallow roasting pan.

13. Fill half of the roasting pan with hot boiling water.

14. Put it in the preheated oven.

15. Bake for 40 – 50 minutes.

16. Turn off the oven.

17. Grease a knife with cooking oil.

18. Run the greased knife around the inside edges of the springform pan.

19. Let the pan stand in the turned-off oven with the door ajar, for 60 minutes.

20. Remove the pan from the oven.

21. Remove it from the roasting pan.

22. Discard the wrapped foil.

23. Put the cheesecake pan in refrigerator for 2 – 3 hours.

To garnish the cheesecake,

24. Mix the marmalade and orange juice.

25. Heat it over low heat to melt the marmalade.

26. To serve,

27. Put the cheesecake on the serving tray.

28. Remove the pan sides.

29. Spread the orange mixture on top of it.

30. Garnish with mint.

Low Fat Pear Cheesecake

Serving Size

Serves 8 – 10

Nutritional Facts (Values per Serving)

Calories/serving: 209

Total Carbohydrate: 35 g

Cholesterol: 58 mg

Total Fat: 2 g

Ingredients

All-purpose flour – 1/3 cups

Low fat cottage cheese – 16 oz.

Dried pears, chopped – 6

Brown sugar – ¼ cup

Low fat cream cheese – 16 oz.

Crystallized ginger – 1/3 cups

Low fat granola – 1 cup

Eggs – 3

Water – Half cup

Sugar – Half cup

Vanilla extract – 2 tsp.

Preparation Method

1. Set the oven to preheat at 325°F.

2. Grease a 9 inch springform pan with cooking oil.

3. Put ginger, pears and water in a saucepan.

4. Bring it to a simmer on low heat.

5. Cover and let it cook for 12 – 14 minutes.

6. While the pears are cooking, blend the granola in a food processor.

7. Press the blended granola evenly in the greased springform pan

8. Now blend the pear ginger mixture in the food processor.

9. Blend till it becomes a smooth puree.

10. Let it cook for 10 minutes.

11. Add cream cheese and cottage cheese in it. Process again for a few minutes.

12. Add the brown and white sugar in the processor. Run the processor till the sugar blends well.

13. Start adding the eggs now. Add one egg at a time while the processor is running.

14. Finally, add the all purpose flour and vanilla extract.

15. Pour this batter in the springform pan.

16. Put it in the preheated oven for 50 – 60 minutes.

17. Turn off the oven.

18. Grease a knife with cooking oil.

19. Run the greased knife around the inside edges of the springform pan.

20. Let the pan stand in the turned-off oven with the door ajar, for 60 minutes.

21. Remove the pan from the oven.

22. Put the cheesecake pan in refrigerator for 3 – 4 hours before serving.

Crunchy Pumpkin Mousse

Serving Size

Serves 8 – 10

Nutritional Facts (Values per Serving)

Calories/serving: 230

Total Carbohydrate: 42 g

Cholesterol: 4 mg

Total Fat: 5 g

Ingredients

Gingersnap cookies – 8 oz.

Raisins – 2 Tbsp.

Canola oil – 1 Tbsp.

Pumpkin puree – 1 cup

Brown sugar – 1/3 cup

Cinnamon powder – ½ tsp

Ground ginger – ¼ tsp

Nutmeg, grated – ¼ tsp

Low fat soft vanilla ice cream – 2 cups

Preparation Method

1. Set the oven to preheat at 350°F.

2. Grease a 9 inch pie pan with cooking oil.

To make the crust,

3. Chop the gingersnaps and raisins in a food processor.

4. Process till both the ingredients are finely chopped.

5. Add oil in the food processor and blend for a few more minutes.

6. Press this mixture evenly in the greased pie pan.

7. Put it in the oven for 10 – 15 minutes.

To make the filling,

8. In a large bowl, mix sugar, ginger, pumpkin puree, nutmeg and cinnamon powder.

9. Add ice cream in the bowl. Mix well.

10. Pour this mixture over the crust in the pie pan.

11. Put it in the refrigerator for at least 2 hours.

Nutty Pear Treat

Serving Size

Serves 7 – 8

Nutritional Facts (Values per Serving)

Calories/serving: 301

Total Carbohydrate: 54.2 g

Cholesterol: 2 mg

Total Fat: 10.2 g

Ingredients

All-purpose flour – 2 Tbsp.

Old fashioned rolled oats – 1 ½ cups

Wheat flour – 1/3 cup

Cinnamon – ½ tsp

Crushed crystallized ginger – 2 Tbsp.

Canola oil – 5 Tbsp.

Walnuts, chopped – Half cup

Anjou pears – 3 ½ lbs.

Maple syrup – Half cup

Brown sugar – Half cup

Raisins – Half cup

Lemon Juice – 2 Tbsp.

Preparation Method

1. Set the oven to preheat at 350°F.

To make the filling,

2. In a large bowl, mix maple syrup, pears, lemon juice, ginger and all purpose flour.

3. Pour this mixture in a deep dish baking pan.

To make the topping,

4. In a bowl, mix rolled oats, brown sugar, walnuts, cinnamon powder and wheat flour.

5. Sprinkle a few drops of oil. Mix well.

6. Spread this topping over the filling in the baking pan.

7. Put it in the preheated oven for 45 – 50 minutes.

8. Let it cool for 10 minutes before serving.

Lavender Strawberries with Cream Dip

Serving Size

Serves 8

Nutritional Facts (Values per Serving)

Calories/serving: 135

Total Carbohydrate: 24.6 g

Cholesterol: 20 mg

Total Fat: 2.8 g

Ingredients

Dried lavender – ½ tsp

Greek yogurt – 16 oz.

Unflavored gelatin – ½ tsp

Honey – ¼ cup

Strawberries, quartered – 2 cups

Sugar – 1/3 cup

Egg yolks – 3

Cornstarch – 2 Tbsp.

Water – 1/3 cup

Low fat milk – Half cup

Pinch of salt

Preparation Method

1. In a saucepan, put water, sugar and dried lavender.

2. Bring the mixture to boil.

3. Stir and cook till the sugar dissolves completely.

4. Turn off the heat and let it sit for 10 minutes.

5. Seep the liquid through a sieve into a bowl.

6. Discard the solid residues.

7. In another small bowl, dissolve gelatin in 1 tablespoon of water.

8. Let it sit for 2 minutes.

9. In another large bowl, whisk together cornstarch, honey, egg yolks and salt.

10. In another saucepan, heat milk over medium heat. Do not boil the milk.

11. Slowly and gradually add the hot milk in the egg yolk and honey mixture while whisking continuously.

12. Pour back this mixture into the saucepan.

13. Cook for 3 minutes over medium heat while stirring continuously.

14. Turn off the heat and add gelatin mixture in it. Stir well.

15. Pour all of it in a bowl.

16. Let it cool for 20 minutes. Keep stirring it so that it does not set.

17. Add Greek yoghurt in it. Mix well.

18. Divide this mixture equally in desert glasses.

19. Top it with a quartered strawberry.

20. Sprinkle about 2 teaspoons lavender-sugar syrup on top of it.

Chewy Fudge Brownies

Serving Size

Serves 12 – 14

Nutritional Facts (Values per Serving)

Calories/serving: 147

Total Carbohydrate: 22.6 g

Cholesterol: 47 mg

Total Fat: 6.2 g

Ingredients

Egg – 1

All-purpose flour – 1 cup

Low fat milk – ¼ cup

Unsweetened cocoa – Half cup

Egg yolks – 2

Dark chocolate, diced – 2 oz.

Butter – 1/3 cup

Sugar – 1 cup

Vanilla extract – approximately 1 tsp

Salt – ½ tsp

Cooking spray to grease the pan

Preparation Method

1. Set the oven to preheat at 350°F.

2. Coat an 8 inches baking pan with cooking spray.

3. In a bowl, mix cocoa, all purpose flour and salt.

4. Put butter and dark chocolate in a microwave safe bowl.

5. Microwave at high for 45 seconds, while stirring after 15 seconds. Set aside to cool.

6. Now add put milk, sugar, vanilla extract, egg and egg yolks in it. Whisk well.

7. Add this mixture in the flour mixture. Mix well.

8. Pour this batter straight into the baking pan.

9. Put it in the preheated oven for 20 – 25 minutes.

Lemon Catalana

Serving Size

Serves 6

Nutritional Facts (Values per Serving)

Calories/serving: 142

Total Carbohydrate: 21 g

Cholesterol: 111 mg

Total Fat: 4.9 g

Ingredients

Fresh lemon rind – 3 strips (3 inch each)

Cornstarch – 2 Tbsp.

Cinnamon stick – 1 (2 inch)

Egg yolks – 3

Whole milk – 2 cups

Sugar – 7 Tbsp.

Pinch of salt

Preparation Method

1. In a saucepan, heat milk over medium heat. Do not boil the milk.

2. Turn off the heat.

3. Add lemon rind and cinnamon in it.

4. Cover the pan and let it sit for 30 minutes.

5. After 30 minutes, discard the cinnamon stick and rind.

6. In a small bowl, add cornstarch, 4 tablespoons of sugar and salt. Mix well.

7. Add ¼ cinnamon-rind flavored milk in it. Mix well.

8. Return this mixture in the milk containing saucepan.

9. Cook over medium heat for 7 – 8 minutes while whisking continuously.

10. In another bowl, put the egg yolks.

11. Pour one-third of the hot milk mixture in it while whisking continuously.

12. Return this mixture to the milk containing saucepan.

13. Cook on low heat for another 5 minutes while whisking continuously.

14. Pour it equally into 6 desert glasses.

15. Cover the glasses with a plastic wrap and put them in the refrigerator for at least 4 hours.

16. Remove the plastic wrap.

17. Sprinkle the remaining sugar equally over the custard.

18. Light a kitchen blowtorch, two inches atop the custard. Heat the sugar for 60 seconds.

19. Serve immediately.

Chocolicious Bundt Cake

Serving Size

Serves 8 – 9

Nutritional Facts (Values per Serving)

Calories/serving: 234

Total Carbohydrate: 46 g

Cholesterol: 13 mg

Total Fat: 5.1 g

Ingredients

Sugar – 1 cup

All-purpose flour – 1 cup

Non-fat buttermilk – 1 cup

Brown sugar – ¾ cup

Unsweetened pumpkin puree – 15 oz.

Whole wheat pastry flour – ¾ cup

Unsweetened cocoa powder – ¾ cup

Baking powder – 1 ½ tsp

Egg white – 1

Baking soda – 1 ½ tsp

Light corn syrup – ¼ cups

Pumpkin pie spice – 1 tsp. (recipe at the end)

Canola oil – ¼ cups

Egg – 1

Vanilla extract – 1 Tbsp.

Pinch of salt

Powdered Sugar – Half cup

Buttermilk – 1 Tbsp. to make the topping

Chocolate chips – 2 Tbsp.

Preparation Method

1. Set the oven to preheat at 350°F.

2. Then Grease a 12-cup Bundt pan with some cooking spray.

3. In a large bowl, add whole-wheat pastry flour, baking powder, baking soda, all-purpose flour, unsweetened cocoa, salt, sugar and pumpkin pie spice. Mix well.

4. In another bowl, put pumpkin puree, 1 cup of buttermilk and brown sugar. Blend it using an electric mixer.

5. Add in a whole egg along with an egg white. Beat well.

6. Now add oil, vanilla extract and corn syrup in it. Mix well.

7. Start adding the flour mixture. Add gradually while stirring continuously.

8. Pour the batter into the greased pan.

9. Put it in the preheated oven for 60 – 80 minutes, or until the center part of the pan comes out without any moist cake attached on it.

10. Let it cook for at least 2 hours.

11. To garnish,

12. Put the cake on the serving tray.

13. In a small bowl, mix the powdered sugar with extra 1 tablespoon buttermilk. Mix well.

14. Drizzle it over the cake.

15. Sprinkle chocolate chips on top while the topping remains moist.

Low Fat Squash Cheesecake

Serving Size

Serves 8 – 10

Nutritional Facts (Values per Serving)

Calories/serving: 146

Total Carbohydrate: 18 g

Cholesterol: 37 mg

Total Fat: 6.2 g

Ingredients

Old fashioned rolled oats – Half cup

Cinnamon powder – ¼ tsp

Sugar – 2 Tbsp. (for crust)

All-purpose flour – ¼ cup (for crust)

Sugar – Half cup (for filling)

All-purpose flour – 3 Tbsp (for filling)

Eggs – 2

Low fat graham crackers – 9

Nonfat milk – 3 Tbsp

Squash puree – Half cup

Unsalted butter – 2 Tbsp.

Low fat cream cheese – 16 oz.

Vanilla extract – 1 tsp

Salt – ¼ tsp

Preparation Method

1. Set the oven to preheat at 350°F.

2. Grease a deep dish baking pan with cooking spray.

To make the crust,

3. Crush the rolled oats, graham crackers, ¼ cup all-purpose flour and two tablespoons sugar in a food processor. Process till all the ingredients are thoroughly crushed.

4. Add milk in it. Process again for a few minutes.

5. Pour out this mixture in the greased baking pan.

6. Press it evenly in the bottom of the pan.

7. Put it in the preheated oven for 10 minutes.

8. Let it cool for 20 minutes.

To make the filling,

9. Reduce the oven temperature to 325°F.

10. In large bowl, beat cream cheese with an electric mixer. Beat till the cream cheese comes smooth.

11. Add squash puree in it and beat well.

12. Beat in 1 egg and then beat in another.

13. Finally, add salt, cinnamon, vanilla extract and 3 tablespoons all-purpose flour. Beat well.

14. Pour this filling over the baked crust.

15. Bake it for 35 – 40 minutes.

16. Let it cool for a while.

17. Put it in the refrigerator for at least 1 hour before serving.

Coconut Flavored Pumpkin Pie

Serving Size

Serves 8 – 10

Nutritional Facts (Values per Serving)

Calories/serving: 260

Total Carbohydrate: 33 g

Cholesterol: 80 mg

Total Fat: 12.6 g

Ingredients for Crust

Unsalted butter, diced into small pieces – 4 Tbsp.

White whole wheat flour – 1 ¼ cups

Sugar – 1 Tbsp.

Low fat cream cheese – 4 Tbsp.

Slivered almonds, toasted – Half cup

Salt – ½ tsp

Ingredients for Filling

Eggs – 3

Canned pumpkin puree – 1 ½ cups

Cinnamon powder – 1 tsp

Sugar – ¾ cups

Ground ginger – ¼ tsp

Ground cloves – ¼ tsp

Dark rum – 2 Tbsp.

Coconut milk – 1 cup

Coconut flakes – 1/3 cup

Preparation Method

1. Set the oven to preheat at 350°F.

2. Grease a deep removable-bottom tart pan with cooking oil.

To make the crust,

3. Add almonds, sugar, flour and salt in the foods processor. Process till the almonds are thoroughly ground.

4. Start adding butter, one piece at a time. Process after adding every piece.

5. Start adding cream cheese, one tablespoon at a time. Process after adding every spoon.

6. Once thoroughly processed, pour it out into the greased pan.

7. Press it evenly into the bottom and all the way up to the sides of the pan.

8. Set it in the preheated oven for 15 minutes.

9. Let it cool for a while.

Meanwhile, prepare the filling. To make the filling,

10. Combine sugar, pumpkin puree, ginger, cinnamon powder, dark run and cloves in a large bowl. Blend using an electric mixer, on low speed.

11. Start adding eggs, one egg at a time. Beat after adding every egg.

12. Now add coconut milk. Beat well.

13. Place the crust filled tart pan on a baking sheet. Pour the filling in it.

14. Bake for 40 – 45 minutes.

15. Let it cool to room temperature before serving.

16. Garnish with coconut flakes.

Crunchy Thanksgiving Cake Delight

Serving Size

Serves 7 – 8

Nutritional Facts (Values per Serving)

Calories/serving: 893

Total Carbohydrate: 92.8 g

Cholesterol: 166.3 mg

Total Fat: 55.4 g

Ingredients

Eggs – 4

White packaged cake mix – 18 oz.

Pumpkin puree – 2 cups

Margarine – 1 cup

Sugar – 1 ¼ cups

Evaporated milk – 12 oz.

Allspice – ¼ tsp

Cinnamon powder – 2 tsp

Walnuts, chopped – 2 cups

Nutmeg – ½ tsp

Salt – 1 tsp

Whipped cream to decorate the cake

Preparation Method

1. Set the oven to preheat at 350°F.

2. Coat a 9 x 13 inch baking pan with cooking spray.

3. In a large bowl, put evaporated milk, sugar, pumpkin puree, eggs, allspice, cinnamon powder, nutmeg and salt. Mix well.

4. Pour it out into the greased baking pan.

5. Spread the cake mix on top of it.

6. Sprinkle the chopped walnuts over it.

7. Top it up with margarine.

8. Put it in the preheated oven for 55 – 60 minutes.

9. Let it cool completely.

10. Pipe the whipped cream over it to decorate as you like.

Creamy Pumpkin Cake Roll

Serving Size

Serves 6 – 8

Nutritional Facts (Values per Serving)

Calories/serving: 382.5

Total Carbohydrate: 52.2 g

Cholesterol: 116.2 mg

Total Fat: 17.5 g

Ingredients for Cake roll

Canned pumpkin - 2/3 cup

Flour - ¾ cup

Eggs – 3

Cinnamon – 1 tsp

Baking soda – 1 tsp

Sugar – 1 cup

Nutmeg – ½ tsp

Powdered sugar to sprinkle over the kitchen towel – as required

Ingredients for Filling

Softened butter, 4 Tbsp

Soft cream cheese – 8 oz.

Powdered sugar – 1 cup

Vanilla extract – 1 tsp

Preparation Method

1. Set the oven to preheat at 350°F.

2. Coat a 10 x 15 inch jelly roll pan with cooking spray.

3. Line the pan with paraffin paper.

4. Grease the paper and sprinkle a bit of flour on it.

5. Beat eggs and sugar in a large bowl.

6. Add in the remaining roll dough ingredients and beat well.

7. Pour this batter into the prepared jelly roll pan.

8. Put it in the preheated oven for 15 minutes.

9. Meanwhile, sprinkle some powdered sugar using a sieve, on a kitchen towel.

10. Once the roll dough is baked, take it out carefully.

11. Put it in the sugar containing tray. Discard the paraffin paper.

12. Sprinkle more powdered sugar over the hot roll cake.

13. Roll up the cake with towel inside and let it cool for at least 30 minutes.

14. Meanwhile, make the filling.

15. Beat all the filling ingredients till it becomes a smooth and creamy paste.

16. Unroll the cake slowly.

17. Spread the filling mixture on it.

18. Roll the cake again with filling inside it.

19. Wrap the roll in a waxed paper and then with foil.

20. Put it in the refrigerator for at least 2 hours.

21. Slice and serve.

Spicy Pumpkin Treat

Serving Size

Serves 3

Nutritional Facts (Values per Serving)

Calories/serving: 1175

Total Carbohydrate: 339 g

Cholesterol: 162 mg

Total Fat: 113 g

Ingredients

Canned pumpkin – half cup

Pecans, chopped – 1 cup

Brown sugar – 1 cup

Evaporated milk – 2/3 cup

Pumpkin pie spice – 2 tsp. (recipe at the end)

Sugar – 2 cups

Butter – ¾ cup

White chocolate chips – 2 cups

Marshmallow cream – 7 oz.

Vanilla extract – 1 ½ tsp

Preparation Method

1. Line a 9 x 13 inches pan with foil.

2. In a large saucepan, add brown sugar, pumpkin, sugar, evaporated milk, butter and pumpkin pie spice. Bring it to a boil while stirring continuously.

3. Keep it boiling for about 10 minutes.

4. Add marshmallow cream, pecans, white chocolate chips and vanilla in it. Stir vigorously for 60 seconds.

5. Pour it in the foil-lined pan.

6. Let it cool for at least 2 hours.

7. Cover it tightly and put it in the refrigerator for another hour.

8. To serve; lift out of the pan, remove the foil and cut into small slices.

Choco Pumpkin Cookies

Serving Size

Makes about 24 cookies

Nutritional Facts (Values per Serving)

Calories/serving: 162.6

Total Carbohydrate: 26.9 g

Cholesterol: 17.9 mg

Total Fat: 5.8 g

Ingredients

Canned pumpkin – 1 cup

Butter – Half cup

Cups flour, sifted – 2 ½ cups

Cinnamon powder – 1 tsp

Sugar – 1 ½ cups

Baking soda – 1 tsp

Chocolate chips – ¾ cup

Egg – 1

Baking powder – ¾ tsp

Nutmeg – 1 tsp

Vanilla extract – 1 tsp

Salt – ¼ tsp

Preparation Method

1. Set the oven to preheat at 300ºF.

2. In a large bowl, beat sugar and butter till it becomes soft and creamy.

3. Add egg, vanilla and pumpkin in it. Beat till it looks slightly curdled.

4. In another bowl, add baking powder, flour, baking soda, cinnamon powder, nutmeg and salt in it. Mix well.

5. Now mix this dry mixture into the cream mixture.

6. Add chocolate chips. Mix well.

7. Scoop out batter into the ungreased baking tray to make the cookies, keeping a sufficient distance between dough scoops. Make sure there is enough space for the cookies to spread while baking.

8. Put the tray in the preheated oven for 20 – 25 minutes.

9. Let it cool for a while before serving.

Breadilicious Pumpkin Pudding

Serving Size

Serves 10 – 12

Nutritional Facts (Values per Serving)

Calories/serving: 184.1

Total Carbohydrate: 38.7 g

Cholesterol: 0.9 mg

Total Fat: 0.8 g

Ingredients

Canned pumpkin – 16 oz.

Whole wheat bread – 8 slices

Pumpkin pie spice – 1 ¼ tsp (recipe at the end)

Eggs, beaten – 3

Nutmeg – ½ tsp

Skim milk – 2 cups

Raisins – half cup

Brown sugar – 1 cup

Cinnamon powder – 1 ½ tsp

Vanilla extract – 1 tsp

Preparation Method

1. Set the oven to preheat at 375°F.

2. Lightly grease a casserole dish with cooking oil.

3. Make bread crumbs by crumbling the bread in a food processor.

4. Add in it eggs, pumpkin, milk, cinnamon powder, brown sugar, vanilla extract, nutmeg and pumpkin pie spice. Mix well.

5. Add raisins. Mix well.

6. Pour this batter into the greased casserole dish.

7. Fill half of a large baking dish with water. Place the casserole dish in the water filled baking dish.

8. Put it in the preheated oven for 55 – 60 minutes.

Low Fat Pumpkin Butter

Serving Size

Make about 2 cups butter

Nutritional Facts (Values per Serving)

Calories/serving: 27.7

Total Carbohydrate: 6.9 g

Cholesterol: 0 mg

Total Fat: 0 g

Ingredients

Canned pumpkin – 1 ½ cup

Sugar – 2 tbsp

Clove – ¼ tsp

Water – ¼ cup

Brown sugar – ¼ cup

Ginger – ¼ tsp

Nutmeg – ¼ tsp

Allspice – ½ tsp

Cinnamon powder – ½ tsp

Preparation Method

1. Except for the canned pumpkin, put all the ingredients in a microwave safe bowl. Mix well.

2. Microwave on high for 3 minutes.

3. Stir all the ingredients.

4. Now add the pumpkin. Mix well.

5. Microwave again on high for 5 minutes. Mix well.

6. Let it cool for a while.

7. Store it in a butter jar or airtight container and put it in the refrigerator.

8. Serve it with bread, pie and other deserts.

Pumpkin Pie Spice

Serving Size

Makes about 4 tablespoons

Nutritional Facts (Values per Serving)

Calories/serving: 6.8

Total Carbohydrate: 1.5 g

Cholesterol: 0 mg

Total Fat: 0.2 g

Ingredients

Ground Nutmeg – 2 tsp

Cinnamon powder - 7 tsp

Ground Clove – 1 tsp

Ginger powder – 2 tsp

Preparation Method

1. Mix all the ingredients and store in a spice container.

Final Words

Now you are all set for the Thanksgiving bash. Plan what you are going to make this year, grab all the required ingredients and celebrate a healthy delicious Thanksgiving with your loved ones.

Have a Happy Thanksgiving!